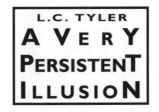

L.C. TYLER

A VERY
PERSISTENT
ILLUSION

Also by L.C. Tyler

The Herring Seller's Apprentice

L.C. TYLER

A VERY PERSISTENT ILLUSION

Macmillan New Writing

First published 2009 by Macmillan New Writing
an imprint of Pan Macmillan Ltd
Pan Macmillan, 20 New Wharf Road, London N1 9RR
Basingstoke and Oxford
Associated companies throughout the world
www.panmacmillan.com

ISBN 978-0-230-71329-1

1 3 5 7 9 8 6 4 2

A CIP catalogue record for this book is available
from the British Library.

Typeset by Intype Libra, London
Printed and bound by MPG Books Ltd, Bodmin, Cornwall

To Keith

Disclaimer

All characters and institutions in this book are fictitious. The tedium of committee work is drawn from life.

Perhaps the most unsettling thought many of us have, often quite early on in childhood, is that the whole world might be a dream; that the ordinary scenes and objects of everyday life might be fantasies. The reality we live in may be a virtual reality, spun out of our own minds . . .

– Simon Blackburn

Reality is merely an illusion, albeit a very persistent one.

– Albert Einstein

1

A Long Way from Horsham,
18 April this Year

Women have many different ways of showing disapproval, only some of which are immediately apparent to men.

A brief study of my girlfriend, who you will meet shortly, has revealed twenty-three quite distinct gradations of dissatisfaction. I have been obliged to catalogue them all. At some stage in the future, the Sorensen-Birtwistle Revised Scale of Girl-Rage will take its rightful place alongside the Richter Scale, the Beaufort Scale and other internationally recognized measures of danger. While mine lacks the precision of the Beaufort Scale, it has greater relevance for the man who does not get out much in hurricanes.

A Number Five, for example, is defined as a noticeable shaking of indoor items, accompanied by rattling noises, but without significant damage to whatever relationship your girlfriend believes you are in. A Number Four, which I sometimes fancifully visualize as dark cobalt storm clouds with blinding flashes of vermillion lighting, has the power to reduce grown men to jelly and can reputedly kill small mammals asleep in their burrows.

And so on.

Fortunately, what is currently being pointed in my direction is only a Number Nineteen: a sort of grey swirling mist of discontent that mendaciously promises, from time to time, to part and reveal its true cause and origin.

Not that I actually need the mist to part and reveal anything. The cause of this Number Nineteen is only too apparent (even to me). We are due at her parents' house, which is still at least an hour's drive away, at eleven thirty – and it is currently ten fifty-five according to the clock on the tasteful walnut dashboard of my classic sports car. In some way that will be explained to me shortly, this is All My Fault. The car ahead of us edges another couple of inches in the direction of Horsham and I slip smoothly into first gear and edge right along with it. The car ahead stops and I expertly bring the MG to a halt a fingerbreadth from its rear bumper. Handbrake on. A quick flick of the gearstick and we are back in neutral. Job done. I think she'll be pretty pleased with that.

'Brilliant,' she says. 'Ramming the car in front will save us at least half a second. You know, what I'd *really* like now is to have to stop and exchange insurance details with an enraged Rolls Royce owner whose car you've just run into while trying to gain a fraction of a millimetre in the queue. God, you're an idiot.'

'Bentley,' I say knowingly.

'What?'

'It's a *Bentley* ahead of us. And I quite deliberately didn't run into it.'

I give her the knowing smile again. She gives me a quick burst of Number Seven, bordering on a mild Six. (Six is more severe than seven on the Sorensen-Birtwistle Revised, for reasons I'll come to.) 'God, you're a idiot,' she tells me.

'I know. You already said. Twice. But thanks for addressing me as God, anyway.'

The traffic starts to move. The back of my hand brushes against her bare leg as I push the custom leather-clad gearstick to the left and forward. She pulls her leg away as if she has been stung, and smoothes her skirt down over it. In spite of the rather good God joke (see above), I am not in favour.

I am therefore unsurprised that there's one of those funny little lulls in the conversation, as we stop and start and stop and start along East Hill. As we pass Wandsworth Town Hall I say: 'That snail's just overtaken us again.' Then to clarify I add: 'I said, that snail's just—'

'God, you're an idiot.'

I don't repeat my God joke because, I feel, if she didn't find it that funny the first time, then it's probably not going to do me much good this time either.

'Looks like a nice day anyway,' I venture cautiously.

'For *whom*?' My girlfriend is one of the only people I know who can deploy grammar as an offensive weapon.

'The sun will be out in a moment,' I say.

'Lunch will be burnt in a moment too.'

Logically, and I'm sure you will agree with me, this is unlikely. If we are down to eat at twelve thirty (and we always are) it is improbable that her mother would judge things so badly as to have already burned the food by five past eleven. I decide not to point this out. My grandmother always said that it takes two to make a quarrel – but then she never met my girlfriend.

She checks her watch – a Rolex, a recent present from her parents – and frowns. The only wise course of action for me is to remain absolutely silent until we reach the Robin Hood roundabout. I am therefore mildly interested to hear myself say: 'So I suppose there's no point in suggesting sex tonight then?'

She turns away from her contemplation of the recently endangered Bentley in front and faces me. After a brief but perfectly judged silence, she hisses: 'What can you possibly think you deserve tonight in view of your conduct so far today?'

Actually I was planning that the sex should be for both of us, but I go for broke and tell her what I think I deserve.

There is a stunned pause, and then she punches me unnecessarily hard on the shoulder. 'Well, we could always try it.' She laughs. 'Just as long as you promise never to do it with anyone else except me.'

I give her the boyish smile.

She leans across and ruffles my hair, which is fashionably short at the moment. 'You may be a grave disappointment to me in many respects,' she says, 'but that is one thing that I can rely on. Unlike Julian, you don't play around with other women. Unlike Jimmy, you don't play around with other men. Uniquely amongst my past and present boyfriends you are not a total bastard. It is your Unique Selling Point. That makes up for a great deal.'

I wonder if now is a good time to tell her about me and Lucy, but I figure . . . no, probably not.

'What is it,' she asks me, 'that makes a man unfaithful?'

The answer, obviously, is 'opportunity'. This is, however, information that men have been keeping to themselves for hundreds of years, and I am not sure that I would be wise to let it slip out now. So I shrug, which she takes to mean that I am entirely incapable of understanding how any man could be unfaithful, rather than that I just can't be arsed to talk about it. She reaches out a hand and ruffles my hair again, which is fine because ruffled hair looks quite good on me.

'I'll give my mother a call to say we'll be a bit late,' she says brightly, as if she has just remembered the existence of mobile phones and their various and several uses. She is quite cheerful chatting to her mother and all seems well – though I assume that I could be 'that moron', who was late picking her up from her flat in Rosebery Avenue and possibly also the brainless one who has been 'driving like a total idiot as usual'. She snaps the phone shut, pleased with herself and no longer entirely displeased with me. 'That's fine. They'll expect us around twelve thirty and we'll eat at one o'clock.' She checks her watch again, but this time simply to admire the well-engineered piece of Swiss technology and the fine gold and steel bracelet. It *is* going to be a nice day. She starts to hum a little tune that I don't recognize, possibly because she is making it up as she goes along. It is at least a happy song and, if it has words, they would almost certainly be about fluffy lambs in the meadow or babies in their cradles. The latter probably. Babies in their cradles occupy an unreasonable and unhealthy percentage of my girlfriend's waking moments. I listen to the hum carefully to see if I am envisaged as the father of any of the babies.

In the meantime I am desperately trying to get all thoughts of Lucy out of my own mind, because they do not belong there today and I must avoid calling my girlfriend (whose name is not Lucy or anything much like it) Lucy.

'Virginia,' I say, carefully practising her name, 'Virginia, do you know what I think?' Suddenly I realize that I've said this only to practise her name and I have no idea what comes next. But I need not have worried.

'Yes,' she interrupts cheerfully, 'since there are a very limited number of things you think about, I almost certainly do know. There is probably nothing about you that would surprise me in the slightest, and today that suits me just fine. Does that cover whatever question you were about to ask?'

'Yes, Virginia,' I say, practising again, while simultaneously looking straight ahead at the traffic, as recommended in the *Highway Code*. 'Yes, it does.'

'Moron,' she says affectionately. She places a hand lightly on my shoulder and kisses me in a way that she imagines will not distract me from the road. Lucy again flashes into my mind and I stray briefly and illegally into the bus lane.

There are, in fact, many things about me that Virginia does not know. For example:

a) I still read both *Viz* and *Loaded*, and have a stash of them on top of my wardrobe.
b) For about four terms when I was in the Third and

Fourth Form, I supported Tottenham Hotspur and
actually nagged my father into taking me to a couple
of matches at White Hart Lane.
c) I have increasing doubts about whether she exists.

If she knew about a) she would merely take it as further
proof of my immaturity and a possible contributory cause to
my inability to develop a meaningful adult relationship –
with anyone in general, but also with women less generally
and with her in particular. Should I happen to blurt it out at
some point (not likely), or should she take to snooping on
top of my wardrobe (very likely), it would not lower me one
jot in her esteem because, in this respect, the dial is sadly
hovering only just above empty. On the other hand, b) rep-
resents dangerous knowledge, which must be kept from her
at all costs. There would, when you think about it, be little
point in raising c) with her.

I give her a sideways glance. Sometimes I look at her and
feel I am seeing her for the first time (rather as you are now):
the dark, silky, shoulder-length hair, the fine even features,
the delicate but determined jaw line. There are one or two
freckles on her cheek. From this angle you can't quite see the
eyes, but they are brown and, at levels Twenty and below
(Sorensen-Birtwistle Revised), warm and reassuring. You can't
see her legs either, but they are the sort of legs you get if you
do exactly the right amount of exercise to get good legs. You
would take all that in and assume that she must have been
school captain and captain of lacrosse, and you'd be dead
right. She was. All of those things.

'Why are you looking at me like that?'

'No reason,' I say. 'I just like looking at you.'

She seems pleased by this and I decide to risk a little music. I give the dial a quarter turn and the radio bursts into life.

'What *is* that rubbish?' she demands.

I identify the band in question. I tell Virginia the names of the individual band members and who the lead singer played for last year.

She gives me a pitying elder-sister look. 'Why do you still find it necessary to know stuff like that?'

'I'm young enough to take an interest,' I say. 'I *like* what bands are doing now.'

'I'm not and I don't,' she says. 'Anyway, they sound like the Cheeky Girls to me. Are you sure they're not?'

'I am and they don't,' I retort.

But I turn the volume down so that it is just a background hum – a cool background hum, obviously, as befits a classic British sports car with a genuine leather gearstick cover.

'Did you book the hotel?' she asks suddenly.

'Naturally,' I say. 'Usual place. One of the rooms with a sea view.'

'If we do what you suggest we do tonight,' she says, 'we won't have much time left to look at the sea.'

'We can always leave the curtains open while we do it,' I say. 'It takes a lot to shock the good folk of Brighton.'

I should explain that, along with always eating at twelve thirty, another family tradition is lying shamelessly to Virginia's parents. As with so many ancient and much-loved customs, its origins are unfortunately lost in the mists of time. At some point in the past, however, we started sneaking away after tea to spend the night at a seedy hotel on the Brighton seafront. Rationalizing our actions, the logic seems to be as follows: Virginia refuses to share a bedroom with me at her parents' house on the grounds that they would be shocked at our sleeping together while still unmarried or even demonstrably *committed*. To avoid any of the possible complications arising from this basic starting point (e.g. running into Virginia's mother while sneaking from one room to another at three o'clock in the morning) we make some feeble excuse for not being able to stay over and drive off, plausibly London-bound, before doing a U-turn onto the M23 and heading south to Brighton for a late dinner and a double bed overlooking the English Channel. The following day we stroll on the beach or over the South Downs and then have lunch at some quasi-rustic pub before driving back to London. As Virginia points out we are, in our little routines, like an old married couple, a remark to which I don't usually risk a reply. Of course, it is all completely unnecessary. Far from worrying about any hanky-panky under their white crocheted bedspreads, Virginia's parents would, I am pretty sure, be perfectly happy if we did it quite openly on the kitchen table, just so long as grandchildren resulted from the act. Nor would they be greatly troubled to know that we had simply called in for lunch with them on our way down to Brighton, which is not an unreasonable destination for a spring weekend break. From their point of view, the entire subterfuge is without value of any kind. But it seems to have some value for Virginia. It may be something to do with her name, which, like mine, is a hard one to live up to. Or perhaps she just wishes to see herself still as Daddy's (or possibly even Mummy's) Little Girl, whose parents really ought to be shocked at such behaviour in one so young. If so, it must be an illusion that she has cherished for many years and is therefore all the more valuable for being a bit of an antique.

The sad fact is that I am Virginia's Last Chance. After the Julian and Jimmy disasters she has invested a great deal of time in trying to shape me into a suitable father of her unborn children. If she were forced to accept that the project had failed, rather than that it was just over-running on time and budget, then motherhood would recede into the improbable distance. This cruel imbalance in our relationship is something that I exploit only when I really have to.

Her parents too appear to see me in much the same light, in that they are invariably pleasant to me, even to the extent of actually seeming to like me. If at any stage in the next fifty years I decide that I'd like parents-in-law, I'll be quite happy to settle for them.

'Thank goodness it's the weekend,' says Virginia, mercifully interrupting my thoughts. 'I can't stand work at the moment. How is it with you?'

'With me?' I feel a completely unreasonable pang of guilt, tinged with blind panic.

'How's that new assistant of yours? What's her name?'

'The new one?'

'Durrr! That's what I said, dumbo. The *new* one.'

'Er . . .' But I'm just stalling for time. There's no way out and the bad men are coming to get me.

'You must know the names of your own staff,' she says

with a despairing shake of the head that does not entirely rule out the possibility that I don't know any of their names. I'm a rat in a trap. What do I say next? Do I lie or tell the truth? Lying is usually best but . . .

'Lucy,' I say with an honest and open smile. 'She's called Lucy.'

A Porsche carving us up as it swerves across lanes to make the next exit enables me to change the subject of conversation, and I am thus able to leave Virginia to her thoughts, which I'm sure are very interesting for her.

But only if she exists, of course. Only if she actually exists.

2

Neuburg, Danube Valley, November 1619

The waiter knocked at the heavy oak door of the chamber. From the other side of the door came a muffled and accented response: 'Go away.' The waiter opened the door and said by way of apology: 'Ham.'

The gentleman was sitting by the closed stove – an imposing blue and white Dutch-tiled cylinder eight feet high – in the far corner of the room. The heat generated by this piece of modern technology reached as far as the doorway, but that was still not enough to melt the snow that covered the small leaded panes of the chamber's only window. The mid-day light in the room, diffused by this translucent covering, was watery, yellowish and not quite of this world. The gentleman's black shoulder-length hair was untidy as though he had been running his fingers through it constantly all morning, which, as it happened, he had been. His long, mulberry-coloured dressing gown was tied carelessly with a cord and his bare feet were sticking straight out in the direction of the warmth. His nose was large and slightly mis-shapen. His beard was trimmed in what seemed to the waiter an excessive and rather effeminate way. In his hand was a bright red ball of wax, which he clutched to his chest as if it had, for him, greater importance than just any ball of wax.

The gentleman seemed at first to be staring at the stove itself, but the waiter then saw that he had his eyes closed as if trying hard to remember something of great consequence. But, reasoned the waiter, nothing as consequential as this fine midday repast. He coughed in an attention-drawing way, and was then obliged to brush his hand swiftly across the ham to remove the resulting specks of spittle. Fortunately the gentleman's eyes were still shut.

This new guest was a rum old cove and no mistake, the waiter decided. He'd pitched up a few days before, saying he needed a room for the night, but the heavy snowfalls, the prospect of impassable winter roads and a frozen and un-navigable river had kept him here. Some were saying he was a soldier. Some were saying he was a schoolmaster. Some were saying he was a Jesuit. Some said he was French, at the very least, and that his name was De Something or Des Something, as French names tended to be. He was foreign anyway, which meant they could charge him just that little bit more.

'*Allez-vous en,*' said the gentleman, without looking up.

The waiter, who did not speak foreign, even for cash, just blinked and stood his ground.

'I said: go away,' repeated the gentleman, still preoccu-pied.

'You ordered ham,' said the waiter, taking the opportunity to inspect it again for any residual bodily fluids. It looked good enough. 'You said to bring a plate of ham to your room later. It's later now.'

The gentleman rubbed his hand across his face and, turning, slowly focused his dark and now open eyes on the plump, greasy individual before him. The waiter smelt faintly, but not altogether unpleasantly, of wood-smoke, rancid goose fat and sour wine: the scent of one who spends much of his time around the kitchen and is not too concerned about spillage.

'Sit down,' the gentleman commanded, without even a passing reference to the ham. 'On that stool.'

A schoolmaster then, thought the waiter with a sigh. He sat down obediently, holding the battered pewter platter awkwardly a little way in front of him. He was not entirely comfortable, but for the moment it was better than being sent out by the cook into the icy streets to buy half a dozen scrawny chickens.

'I should like your views as a philosopher,' said the gentleman.

'I'll do my best, Your Worship,' said the waiter, unsure of himself but hoping that playful banter might increase the size of his tip. 'Though I must admit I haven't had much time for philosophy of late; I tend to specialize more in washing pots, running errands and getting beaten by the cook. Also taking ham to gentlemen in their chambers, who then apparently don't want it. And accepting *a trifle for my trouble*, if the gentlemen are kind enough. Still, I'll try anything once.'

'Look at the plate in front of you,' said the gentleman, blandly sidestepping any pecuniary digressions. 'How do I know that is ham?'

'Of course it's ham. It's what you ordered. When you get your bill it will say: "Plate of Ham, one florin. *Excluding* service."' The waiter winked.

'So that's the only way I'll know it's ham – because that is what it says on the bill?'

In this inn, yes, thought the waiter. 'Well, it looks like ham, doesn't it?' he said encouragingly.

'But our eyes can deceive us, can they not?' asked the gentleman. 'Have you never thought that you saw your friend Hans in the distance, and then approaching closer the person proved to be a total stranger?'

'No.'

'Really?'

'I don't know anyone called Hans,' said the waiter.

'Fritz?'

'No.'

'Otto?'

'No.'

'Wilhelm?'

'No.'

'Heinz?'

'No.'

'Adolph?'

'No.'

'Ulrich?'

'No.'

'Engelbert?'

'No.'

'Leopold?'

'No.'

'Wolfgang Amadeus?'

'No.'

'Who the hell do you know, then?'

'Carl. Though I don't know him that well.'

'All right – have you never thought that you saw your casual acquaintance *Carl* in the distance, and then approaching closer . . . et cetera et cetera?'

'Yes,' said the waiter. 'Yes, I've done that, and I do get your general drift. I agree our eyes can deceive us but—'

'So, next, does that object on the plate smell like ham, eh?'

The waiter cursed under his breath. So that was what this was all about. He'd told the cook that the ham was off, but would he listen? Just give it to him, the cook had said; the French will eat anything – snails, frogs, tripe – nothing's too odd or smelly for them. Now they were in deep trouble, and it would not be just the cook who ended up in the pillory in the main square for serving rotten meat. And winter was a bad time to spend a day outdoors with your neck between two planks of cold, hard wood.

'If you've changed your mind,' he began, 'we've got some very good beef . . .'

But, strangely, the gentleman was just pressing ahead with his lecture. 'How do I know this little red ball is wax?' asked the gentleman.

So it wasn't about the ham then. 'That's best sealing wax,

that is,' said the waiter, on slightly firmer ground with non-perishable items.

'Of course. And I can tell that it is wax because it is hard and round and smells like wax and makes a certain sound when I tap it. But if I melt it in front of this stove it will no longer be hard or round or make the same noise – and yet it is the same wax as before.'

'Obviously,' said the waiter. 'That's how it is with wax. Ham's a bit different, of course. Leave ham in front of a warm stove – as this probably was, in fact – and—'

'You see,' the gentleman continued, ignoring the interesting parallels between philosophy and grocery, 'all of our senses can deceive us – sight, hearing, smell, touch. We can have dreams so vivid that we believe them to be real. How can you tell now that you are awake rather than dreaming?'

'I could pinch myself,' offered the waiter, generously.

'But how would you know that you were not dreaming the pain?'

'I could kick myself as well. That would hurt more.'

'You could dream that too.'

'I could gouge both my eyes out with an auger.'

Yes, why don't you try that? thought the gentleman. That might be an interesting experiment in practical philosophy.

'Sir, you are clearly an empiricist,' said the gentleman. 'We have to assume, however, that the dream you are currently having is so vivid that you can experience, or think you experience, all of the pains and pleasures that you would when awake. Have you experienced pleasure while you were asleep?'

'Might have done,' said the waiter guardedly.

'You see, when we are dreaming we simply cannot tell we are dreaming, even if the very thought should occur to us in our dream. Perhaps you have had a dream where you dreamt you were dreaming, then dreamt you had woken up?'

'How did you know that?' asked the waiter.

'Everybody has that one,' said the gentleman with a dismissive wave of the hand. 'Of course, eventually we do awake from sleep, but there is another sort of dream from which many do not – I mean madness. You will have seen wretches dressed in rags who believe nonetheless that they are emperors wearing purple robes, holding the world in their sway. Or that their heads are pumpkins or that they are made of glass. So I sit here looking at that ham, thinking I am in a warm room in a hostelry in Neuburg, close to the frozen Danube, but I could be dreaming or I could be mad.'

'I'm mad too, then, because that's where I think I am. Actually, I've never been anywhere else, except Oberhausen, which frankly is not worth the journey. They smell funny and overcharge you for bad food. Now Paris, say, or Peru . . . I'd be prepared to believe they don't exist, never having seen or wanted to see either, but Neuburg is the real thing. And Oberhausen, to the extent I can tell. I'm not sure you're right about madmen thinking they are made of glass though. The ones I have met have just looked at me sideways and talked to themselves. They never mentioned what sort of clothes they thought they were wearing, and I never thought to ask. Of course, if one of them said he wasn't sure he existed, then I'd take that as proof that he was a loopy as a . . . But from the way that Your Excellency is tapping that ball of wax on the table, I fear that I may have missed Your Excellency's point.'

'My *point*,' said the gentleman, transferring the ball of wax quickly to his other hand and taking a deep breath, 'was simply that madmen are also often deceived about reality. The purple robes, pumpkins and so forth and so forth were merely examples of things madmen might imagine. I don't spend a lot of time talking to the mentally deranged. Usually.'

'And *my* point,' said the waiter, keeping a careful eye on the ball of wax, just in case it started tapping again, 'is that I am not mad. Hence, what I say is true and you may accept my word that you are not mad and that you are a fortunate guest in the best inn in Neuburg.'

'Thank you for that reassurance. But even that does not provide the certainty I require. I understand what you appear to be saying to me, but perhaps you too are a figment of my imagination.'

'Or maybe you're a figment of mine,' muttered the waiter, who had been called various things but never previously a figment.

The gentleman snapped his fingers (the hand that no longer held the ball of wax). 'Exactly!' he exclaimed. 'Now you are starting to make progress in philosophy.'

'So, now I am a philosopher, I can't be certain of anything then? Not that it's cold?'

'No.'

'Or that there is daylight through that window?'

'No.'

'Or whether this ham is off?'

'I could smell the ham was off as soon as you brought it into the room, you idiot. But from a purely philosophical viewpoint – no.'

'So, apart from the ham – sorry about that – there's nothing we can be certain of?'

'I can doubt everything except one thing. Do you know what that is?'

'You said: it's the ham.'

'The one thing that I cannot doubt is doubt itself. For the doubt to exist there must be something or someone to do the doubting. *Dubito ergo sum.*'

'Is that French?'

'Latin. "I doubt therefore I am." Or perhaps "think" would be better. *Cogito ergo sum*: "I think, therefore I am." But – and I'll work out the exact phrase later – the one thing I can be certain of is my own existence. On that solitary rock of certainty, my friend, it is possible to construct a whole new philosophical system. Or at least it would be if I didn't have my train of thought broken by people bringing me rancid ham.'

'Well, fancy that,' said the waiter, who had known all along that he existed and did not need a philosopher to tell him. 'The cook, however, will be starting to doubt my existence, so if you will excuse me, Monsieur De . . .'

The gentleman either did not notice or did not care that the waiter had forgotten his name. He offered no assistance in any case.

'So, if you'll excuse me, Monsieur Des . . . Anyway,' said the waiter as he backed through the doorway, still clutching the plate of ham, 'the cook is preparing chicken for supper tonight, which I am sure will compare favourably with anything you would find in Paris.'

The door closed none too softly.

'I doubt that,' said Descartes.

3

Euston Road, 20 April this Year

My first objective on a Monday morning is to get from Great Portland Street station to my office without meeting any of my staff. I do not actively dislike any of them (though I am not sure why I shouldn't) but from the moment the first of them engages me in conversation, the weekend is over and the working week has begun. By sneaking from the train and keeping close to the tiled wall as I follow the crowd up the smooth concrete steps, I can sometimes delay the start of Monday by a good ten minutes. Today, however, I am out of luck. I have hung back to avoid June (not strictly speaking my staff, but very likely to talk to me all the same) only to feel a tap on my shoulder. It is Narinder, my International Assistant.

'Hello, Chris, I thought it was you,' he says triumphantly. He looks so pleased I almost feel sorry for him.

'No, it's somebody else. That's me over there,' I reply.

Narinder looks puzzled for a second, then says: 'Always joking, eh, Chris?'

I agree that I have made a joke and that I am in fact more

or less where I appear to be. He smiles. I actually quite like Narinder, even if he has just shortened the weekend.

Narinder got the job of International Assistant because the selection panel thought that, coming from India or thereabouts, he must know something about international affairs. Actually, he was born in Romford and has never been further than Benidorm, which he hated.

'Good weekend?' I ask. It's the standard question being asked all over central London at this instant. Most people are replying: 'OK, and yourself?'

Narinder, however, is saying: 'Awful, man, just awful. My parents are on at me again about going and staying with my auntie and uncle in Amritsar for a month, you know? What do I want to go there for? I won't know anyone. It's too hot. There's no McDonald's. And it will be all my annual leave taken in one go. I've got other things to do, man. Know what I mean?'

I can take this town or leave it, but Narinder is a Londoner, born and bred. He can survive only on proper English food – curry, pasta, pot noodles, kebabs, hamburgers, French fries. He thinks Glasgow is 'abroad'.

'There's probably a McDonald's in Amritsar,' I say, thinking of McDonalds that I have encountered in Hong Kong, Bangkok, Oslo and even Paris.

'Yeah?'

'Probably.'

For a moment it looks as though this might be enough to clinch the deal; then he shakes his head. 'No, I'm not going to risk it.'

This is his joke, just as mine was mine. Narinder's quite

funny in his own quiet way. There's certainly a risk in going to Amritsar, and we both know what it is, because we've talked about it before. It has nothing to do with hamburgers.

But I just nod. I too am against unnecessary risks.

We have reached the traffic lights and conversation stops abruptly as we run across the road before the traffic starts moving again. When I was younger I used to have this theory that, if you ran across just as the lights were about to change and if you could get to the other side before the stationary red figure replaced the green walking one, then Everything Would Be All Right. What 'Everything' was varied, of course, from time to time. The earliest 'Everything' that I can recall had something to do with an incomplete geography project that I had to hand in that afternoon. Later it encompassed job applications, England winning the World Cup and completely successful contraception. It worked for the geography project (the teacher was absent with flu that afternoon) but its predictive value subsequently was patchy (England inexplicably did not win the World Cup in spite of a number of successful crossings). This time we get across just before the pedestrian lights change, so everything will clearly be All Right for one or other of us.

The Royal Society for Medical Education is in one of those improbably big white houses overlooking Regent's Park. My office, with a sign on the door saying: *'Director of External Affairs'*, is on the highly prestigious first floor, along with such big cheeses as the President and the Secretary. The library and lecture theatre are on the ground floor. Lesser departments such as Continuing Professional Development and Examinations, and also some of the committee rooms, occupy the upper floors. IT is obviously in the base-ment. But I am on the highly prestigious first floor. My staff are clustered around me, their desks packed tightly but ran-domly into a sort of outer office that must once have been half of a grand drawing room – Narinder (International), Fatima (my PA), Jon (Press) and now Lucy (Parliamentary Officer). As I exchange a few cheerful words with each, Monday settles on my shoulders like a damp and malodor-ous horse blanket. I want to weep at the tedium and point-lessness of the next five days, but what I actually say is: 'OK, boys and girls – team meeting at zero nine thirty precisely. Be there or be square. Let's kick Monday in the pants.'

I close my door behind me, groan, slump into my chair, groan again and switch on my computer. As it boots up I try to think of any good reason why I should invite Lucy into my office for a one-to-one discussion on anything. I can't. I scan the BBC website for parliamentary news items but there is nothing that might remotely concern the cool and wacky world of medical education. Nothing at all. As usual the external world seems unaware of our activities or even our existence. Explaining what the Society does, how necessary we are, why academic medicine would crumble if we did not offer grants, run our courses and our diploma examination, lobby tirelessly for medical education and so on and so on – explaining all of that is my job. And, like I say, the entire planet seems unaware that we exist. Excellent. Well done, Chris.

I turn to my emails. I have been sent one hundred and two over the weekend. *One hundred and two.* Don't these people have lives? Evidently not.

I hate Mondays.

But at least on this particular Monday I have lunch with Lucy to look forward to (good) and am meeting Fat Dave for a drink after work (good-ish). I wonder whether they are also, at this moment, looking forward to seeing me. I find it difficult to imagine any of them when I am not there. Of course, I tell myself that somewhere out there they are alive and doing the usual mundane things, starting their own Monday mornings. Somewhere out there the Queen is alive and doing her mundane things, starting her Monday morning. Somewhere out there the Prime Minister is alive and doing something, starting his Monday morning. I know that in the past twenty-four hours the Prime Minister must have eaten approximately three meals, visited the toilet (say) six times, cleaned his teeth at least twice, picked his nose surreptitiously . . . and yet I have great difficulty *visualizing* any of it. Dave will have cleaned his teeth less and picked his nose more, but in all other respects I have the same problem with him. If I were told that, once out of my sight, he was put away in a box for safekeeping until I needed him again, is that any less bizarre than the idea that he has a responsible job with Camden Council and is allowed to make actual decisions? I think not. No, really, I think not.

Nine thirty. Let's get Monday started then.

* * *

There are several good reasons for weekly team meetings:

    a) They are a type of feudal homage paid by my staff to me because, though they all hate and resent the

meetings, I can command them to be there. I like
that.

b) They enable me to consolidate my power base in the
Great Contest with Putrid Passmore for the post of
Deputy Secretary.

c) They allow me to communicate, encourage, exhort,
raise or lower morale and so on and so forth, to the
extent that seems advisable and good to me at any
given time.

'OK, boys and girls,' I say, leaning back in my chair. 'Let's
see what delights await us this week.' The four of them
smile, as they are contractually obliged to do when I say anything that they think that I think might be funny. 'First,' I
continue genially, 'did you all get my email on job plans?'

They all look blank.

'The email on job plans?' I repeat, as if to a group of elderly and rather dim aunts.

'Did you press SEND?' asks Narinder. 'Do you remember
last time you pressed SAVE and . . .'

I'm sure I hear Jon snigger but when I look in his direction he is stony faced and flicking though his diary, one
eyebrow slightly raised. He is wearing a cream shirt and a
loosely knotted paisley tie. The shirt is perfectly ironed,
which is something that happens to you when you are married. (I have a good stock of non-iron shirts.)

'OK,' I say, 'if none of you got my email, then clearly it
is some sort of general system fault. I'll resend it later. In the
meantime, let me summarize Humph's words of wisdom on
job plans . . .'

'Humph?' asks Lucy brightly. She is keen and wishes to learn, as the young of most species are and do.

'He means Roger,' says Narinder. 'The Secretary. Chris refers to him as Humph.'

'Everybody calls him Humph,' I say.

'No, Chris,' says Jon, 'only you call him Humph.'

'Why?' asks Lucy. She is wearing a very tight, baby-pink cashmere sweater that, frankly, ought to be illegal, and I am struggling to focus on her words.

'Because of his resemblance to Sir Humphrey Appleby,' I explain patiently.

'Who?' asks a voice from just above the pink cashmere sweater.

'You're too young to remember,' says Jon, who is certainly old enough, and (I notice) starting to go a bit grey. That too happens to you when you get married.

'*Yes Minister*,' I explain.

Jon nods. 'Sir Humphrey was the Permanent Secretary. Jim Hacker was the Minister.'

'Oh,' says Lucy. But she still hasn't a clue what any of us are on about.

'I'll show you the videos some time,' I offer. 'I have every episode on DVD.'

'Oh, it was a *television* programme then?'

'Moving onwards,' I say with a broad smile to all, 'Jon, what is in your diary this week?'

I lean even further back in my chair, not listening to the series of rather dull tasks that Jon has in store for him, but wondering which evening I should suggest to Lucy for her and her tight cashmere sweater to view one of the nation's best-loved political comedies. I know that Virginia is tied up on Thursday, so Thursday it may well be. We'll obviously need to drink plenty of alcohol while we watch. I'll get in a bottle or two of Chardonnay.

I realize that the room has gone silent and that everyone is looking at me. 'Thanks, Jon,' I say, re-entering the real world. 'That was every bit as interesting as usual.' I pause to show this remark was quite funny, but only Fatima smiles, and she clearly does not understand what the joke was supposed to be. She never does. 'Anything you need help from me with?' I add, to show that I am really supportive, caring, and so on and so forth.

Jon sighs and shakes his head. 'Only, as I *said*, Chris, it would be good if you could get the IT people to fix that software for us. I've tried, but they're not listening to me. Maybe they'll do it if you talk to them.'

'Ah, yes, that,' I say, closing my eyes for a moment and clasping my hands, as if in prayer. 'Thank you, God. The useless-database project. Another screw-up by Corporate Services and another nail in the coffin of Putrid Passmore's hopes to be Deputy.'

'I'd be happy just to have the software fixed quickly,' says Jon, 'if that's OK with you, Chris.'

'I'll speak to Putrid Passmore,' I say.

'That's Brindley Passmore,' says Jon, turning to Lucy. 'Director of Corporate Services. And no, Chris, everyone does *not* call him that. Nor in fact did you before they announced this new Deputy post.'

'Anything else?' I ask tartly. One of the rules of weekly team meetings is that only I can score points.

'Yes,' says Jon, swivelling in his chair, the better to address us all, 'I may as well report, as your union rep, that we have finished negotiating for private healthcare cover for all staff. You can now all fall sick without fear of having to cross the threshold of an NHS hospital.' Jon smiles at us. Pretty well everyone who takes the Society exams, and pretty well everyone who is a member of the Society, works or has worked in the National Health Service. Jon too can make jokes.

'Couldn't you have got us free gym membership?' I ask, winking at Lucy. I don't go to the gym personally, but I'd rather like people to think I might be in there pumping iron from time to time. 'I mean, private health insurance is great when you think you might need to replace a hip or two, or get checked out for dementia, but the younger people here are not going to find it such a great attraction.'

'We carried out a survey of *all* staff,' Jon begins, running fingers through the greying hair, but I dismiss him and the whole boring subject with a wave of my hand.

'Moving on,' I say brightly. And I call on Narinder to tell us about his plans for the week, because I have the power to make him do that.

* * *

'Still here?' asks Humph (as everybody calls him). 'Your colleagues all seem to have gone home.' He stands, a little stiffly – almost shyly – at the doorway of my office. He is unsure if he is disturbing important work, and I am not planning to tell him that he isn't. He is, as usual, dressed in a pinstriped suit (a grey one today) and some stripy tie that will tell the initiated which school or college he was at back in the Dark Ages. He is much too polite to enter my sanctum uninvited. He looks tired. They say he's always in at seven thirty, though I've noticed some days lately he hasn't been in at all. He is usually the last to leave, anyway. He needs a deputy. Let's be specific – he needs me as his deputy.

'I'm meeting somebody later,' I say by way of explanation. I have told Dave I can't get away until seven – people with important jobs obviously should not be seen, as Dave generally is, sitting around in a pub at three nanoseconds past five. As it happens, I am currently running an important Google search to see how many times I can find a reference to myself on the Internet. (Three so far – all Society press releases posted on our own website. Also a school in California and lots of people in Denmark with the same name as me, none of which counts.) Still, I am listed, therefore I exist.

'Can I come in for a second?' Humph asks.

I kill Google with a furtive click of the mouse and say: 'Be my guest.' I narrowly avoid adding 'Humph'.

Humph enters, bringing with him just the faintest trace of some traditional English aftershave. 'It's George,' he begins, twisting a gold cufflink thoughtfully.

'Professor George Magwitch,' I say, 'distinguished, if somewhat outspoken, clinician. Faked his research and now hounded by the press over his dodgy evidence in the Smith case. Former Vice-President of this ancient and august Society.'

Humph looks even more tired than before. 'Distinguished clinician, *cleared* of unfounded accusations concerning his research and briefly criticized by the media for *doing his duty*

31

and giving evidence against elder-abusing care-home staff and Dan Smith in particular. Former Vice-President of the organization that pays you, and don't you forget it. That's the one you're probably thinking of.'

'What's he done now?'

'Nothing, thank goodness. He's been keeping his head down, looking after his patients and saving lives,' says Humph. 'But the criticisms made of him and the evidence he gave still rankle. He now wants to tell his side of the story to the press.'

'Is that wise? They'll have him for breakfast. The press have lost interest in the Smith case. If George talks, they'll only dig out all the old press cuttings on the research. He'd be better off keeping quiet.'

'No, it is not wise,' says Humph, now fingering the stripy tie. (Red and blue. Balliol? As if I gave a monkey's.) 'It would be very brave, but not wise. Anyway, things have moved on. When Dan Smith was cleared of wrongdoing in spite of George's expert testimony, it looked as if that was that. Smith probably had a case against the care home for wrongful dismissal, but it wasn't our problem. Now it seems that Smith is being persuaded to report George to the GMC for giving an inaccurate and biased account of injuries suffered by the inmates – which the court has ruled were nothing to do with Smith and a lot to do with poor management of the home generally. Of course, his claim of bias is nonsense – George just reported factually on the injuries – and I'm sure the GMC *will* throw it out; but, nevertheless, this is not a good time for him to go shooting his mouth off to the press.'

'We can't help it,' I say.

I have to stop the action at this point and explain that my conversations with Dave rest on the interesting premise that we are both irresistible Lotharios with the sex drive and stamina of a stud bull and a *fin de siècle* contempt for the norms of bourgeois society. I am not sure why, other than that maintaining this fiction is more interesting than talking about football all the time.

'So, did you see the match?' asks Dave.

'A bit,' I hedge. 'On Sky.'

He looks at me oddly. 'A *bit*? What sort of Arsenal fan are you?'

'Arsenal till I die, mate,' I say. 'Arsenal till I die. Cut me and I promise you I'll bleed red. And even if I wasn't there to cheer my lads on, it was a great result.'

'*Your* lads? Bet you don't even know the score,' he says. He's a season-ticket holder and I am just an occasional visitor to the Emirates Stadium. He does actually have the right to sneer.

'Two nil,' I say confidently.

'And the scorers?' He raises an eyebrow.

'Henry and . . . er . . . Pires,' I say.

'Would that be the same Pires that we sold to Villarreal last summer?' he asks.

'Could be,' I say.

'It was Van Persie and Clichy,' he says with a shake of his head. 'Jesus, are you some sort of closet Spurs supporter or something?'

'No, but thank you for calling me Jesus.'

'Do you know how often you make that so-called joke?'

'Southend lost again,' I say quickly. Southend are Dave's Other Team, and he's followed them since he was about three. These days he is an occasional visitor to Roots Hall in the same way that I am to the Emirates, but he does the whole Southend thing, including buying the grotty away shirt and hating Colchester. As you know, whichever football team you support, you get to hate one other team, free of charge. Arsenal fans hate Spurs. Celtic fans hate Rangers. Man City fans hate United. If you support Southend, you are allowed to hate Colchester United, which is a nice bonus but doesn't really compensate (in my opinion) for having to support Southend week in, week out. Colchester fans in their turn have a chant that goes:

> *We hate Southend and we hate Southend*
> *We hate Southend and we hate Southend*
> *We are the Southend haters.*

'Yeah, they got stuffed,' he says, but with less feeling than when he was talking about Paul and Megan.

'Colchester look set for promotion,' I add, wondering if it is possible to twist the knife just a bit more. Like I say, Dave's a good mate.

'No, they don't.' He shakes his head again. 'One sports writer said they were good enough for the Premiership, now everybody is jumping on the bandwagon and tipping them to be promoted. Confucius, he say – where one dog pisses, many dogs shall piss.'

The sayings of Confucius are another one of our regular games. Some sayings like: 'Man not buy round, good friend spit in his beer' (one of mine) are funny only when you've

had so much to drink that almost anything is funny. Oth
like: 'Where one dog pisses, many dogs shall piss' (one
Dave's) are surprisingly true at all sorts of levels.

'If you are going to talk about important stuff,' D
continues, 'at least get your facts right. Colchester los
Saturday and all Colchester fans are going to hell by
Wednesday morning. Thus is it is written. Whose roun
anyway?'

'Yours,' I say.

'What are you having? A pint of Shires?' This is
Dave's boring so-called jokes, Shires being a fictitiou
ery from a soap opera about farming folk.

'Time for a Tiger,' I say, which is an obscure lite
erence as well as an instruction to get me some
refreshment.

'Tiger it is then, mate,' says Dave, completely
by his close brush with culture.

He waddles off, piloting his large frame expert
the crowd and onwards towards the bar. Dav
exhibit grace under most circumstances, but wh
ting in his round he's a nice little mover.

I probably should be with Virginia this ev
ing in mind I'm planning to two-time her
(an arrangement firmed up with Lucy over lun
thinks, however, that Dave is an immature sl
influence on me, so avoids these little get-togeth
ing of Fat Dave reminiscing on, say, Ian Wr
goals or the ten grossest things he has seen at t
necessarily on the screen), would result in

least bring on a potentially fatal Number Two (Sorensen-Birtwistle Revised).

Fat Dave (Birtwistle) is the joint inventor of the Sorensen-Birtwistle Revised Classification and is personally responsible for its chief imperfection, namely that the most lethal form of disapproval is the so-far undiscovered and purely hypothesized Number One. Number One is defined as Virginia actually physically killing me on the spot. Number Two (also as yet unencountered in real life) entails my hospitalization for greater than forty-eight hours and possible lingering demise. And so on and so on, as I may have observed before. Twenty-Three is disapproval so mild as to be unnoticeable by a third party and during which sexual intercourse is theoretically possible. The problem, as you will see, is that we should have started with zero as being total calm and worked our way upwards, with an infinite number of higher degrees of girl-rage available to us. We have, for example, no numbers left to cover Virginia running amok and murdering both me *and* Dave, which we definitely should have allowed for. But the Sorensen-Birtwistle Revised is now so long established (seven or eight months) that to change it would be immensely confusing for either of us, particularly when we are drunk, as we usually are when we get round to using the scale in earnest. We'll need another beer or two before we start on that topic tonight.

'There you go,' says Dave, slamming the open and foaming bottle down on the table. 'So when are you next seeing Virginia?'

'Weekend,' I reply, mistiming a suck and feeling the ice-

cold beer drip from my chin. I blame Dave. 'You've shaken this beer up, you silly tart.'

'No, it's just that after two sips, you're already too drunk to know where your mouth is.'

I mime hilarious and uncontrollable laughter. But I am ignored.

'Shouldn't you tell her?' Dave says, as if returning to an earlier subject.

'Tell her what?'

'About Lucy.'

'Nothing to tell,' I say.

'You'll come unstuck,' he says.

'I'm not stuck, so I can't come unstuck,' I say.

'Moron,' he says.

'Sorry, Dave, I can't *quite* put my finger on it, but something tells me you don't approve, do you?'

'Not up to me, mate,' he says in a way that suggests that it is really. 'But if I had a girlfriend like Virginia . . .'

There is a long contemplative pause during which we just drink with focused, deadly accuracy and don't look at each other that much.

'Whose round is it?' asks Dave.

'Yours,' I say.

* * *

'Spain,' says a bored voice at the distant end of the phone.

'Hi, Digby! It's Chris. Chris Sorensen,' I say.

There is a pause as though somebody is quickly riffling through a card index or similar.

'Ah . . . Christian Sorensen, Royal Society for Medical

Education . . . yes, of course . . .' There is another pause, then a cautious: 'So, how can I help you exactly?'

'It's George Magwitch,' I say.

'Inevitably,' says Digby Spain. There is another pause. I don't remember him being quite this laconic before.

'You were very supportive of him over the faked-research issue.'

'It wasn't faked,' he says quickly. 'Others misused his data. Others misquoted him. But his original research stands up to scrutiny. I was happy – my newspaper was happy – to be able to set the record straight, and I was grateful to you for the briefing you gave us.'

'He wants to set the record straight again. This time he wants to talk to you himself. The court cleared Dan Smith, but that does not necessarily mean that Professor Magwitch's evidence against him was in any way biased or at fault. It doesn't amount to the gross-misconduct charge Smith is threatening to bring.'

'Not sure I can necessarily help you this time, Christian. I've already told—'

'He wants to talk to a journalist,' I interrupt, before we start to get too negative. 'Somebody we know and whose impartiality we can trust. I'd like him to talk to you. Exclusively to you.'

'And he's actually willing to do that?'

'He will be. I'll speak to him and give him your number.'

There is another long pause.

'You know, Christian, I can't promise how this will come out. I can only talk to him and make up my own mind.'

'A lot of people have made up their minds already. All

I'm asking, Digby, is that you give him a fair hearing. From what you wrote before I think we can rely on your integrity.'

'Fine.'

'Fine?'

'Tell him to call me. I'll see what I can do.'

I breathe a sigh of relief. 'I won't forget this,' I say.

'Possibly not,' he replies.

4

Wonderful West Sussex Again, 25 April this Year

Virginia's family are ordinary. It is possible that, at some stage in the past, they set out quite deliberately to become the typical middle-class English family. If so, they got commendably close.

Her father worked for years for a medium-sized insurance company before retiring, averagely early, to a medium-sized town halfway along the south coast. They live in one of those nice semis in one of those nice roads that you can find in any town in the South of England – mock Tudor, overblown tea roses in the flint-walled front garden, ruthlessly weeded, spirit-levelled lawn at the back, well-oiled mower in the tidy garden shed. You can tell that he considers himself a bit of a lad but, the moment you saw him, you'd know that his idea of risk taking would be to claim for two cups of coffee on his expenses when the rules said he could claim for one. And then he'd probably lose sleep over it. He's the sort of person you'd trust. He's the sort of person you'd want looking after your insurance, in the days when insurance was what he did. He's been careful with his own money too. He can't have earned that much with the company he worked for, but he managed to pay to send Virginia to a good school and to buy a nice house in an expensive town – and, now I come to think about it, to purchase the occasional Rolex for members of his family. It just shows that honesty can sometimes pay.

These days he has an adequate pension and amuses himself with military history. He was, at some time, briefly in the Suffolk Regiment and writes occasional articles for specialist journals on that and related matters. He has been working for the past fifteen years on a guide to the battlefields of England, and family holidays have long been thoughtfully located in bits of countryside that were worth fighting over. He does not do casual unless you count a sports jacket and tweedy tie as casual.

Daphne, Virginia's mother, worked as a secretary for the same insurance company until she married Virginia's father and was thereafter able to devote the rest of her days to hand-rearing Virginia into what she is today. Virginia was their only foray into childbearing, suggesting either that they thought they'd hit the jackpot first time, or that they thought they had missed it by so much that it wasn't worth having another punt.

Daphne is quite short, quite plump, and can usually be found smiling at somebody or something with absent-minded curiosity. Her main mission in life these days is to remember where she put her reading glasses. I have never heard either of them utter a disparaging word to each other or to any third party, which makes you wonder where Virginia gets it all from. One day I shall ask them whether she was left on their doorstep in a bundle of rags by a passing troop of gypsies.

But I shall not ask them today.

Yes, it's another Saturday and another drive down to Horsham. Today we are on time and there is almost no tension at all in the car as we leave the A24 at Broadbridge Heath and head into town. We are in Sussex only for the day because Virginia has some work thing to go to tomorrow in London and a booking at the dodgy but tolerant Brighton hotel with a heavy-duty bed is therefore not required. Virginia seems relaxed – almost radiant. I have remembered both to buy and actually to bring her father's birthday present. Nothing can go wrong.

'So, Hugh,' I say to Virginia's father, once all of the greetings are out of the way and the birthday present (for Tuesday) and the bottle of wine (for today, unless he has something better in stock, hopefully) are being handed over. 'So, Hugh, what are you working on at the moment?'

'It's a piece for *History Today* on the Minden Regiments,' he says, straightening his tie. 'An important anniversary is coming up, as you know.'

'12th Foot, 20th Foot, 23rd Foot, 25th Foot, 37th Foot, 51st Foot,' I say, ticking them off on my fingers (with a tricky switch to the other hand, still clutching the bottle, for the 51st Foot).

Out of the corner of my eye, I see Virginia mouthing 'brown-nose' at me and casting her eyes towards the ceiling. Hugh just says: 'Quite so.' He thinks everyone ought to know who the Minden Regiments are and that most people do.

Over lunch, Hugh explains (and not for the first time) his admiration of Napoleon. The little Corsican is one of those characters who appeals to the most unlikely people. There's nothing in Hugh, to look at him, that would make you think he would like to set himself up as emperor or invade Russia in the winter, but he clearly thinks well of people who do these things.

'It was his ability to carry out the bold and completely unexpected move,' Hugh is saying, 'at least in his early battles. Wellington was a journeyman by comparison – the slow, careful build-up, plenty of reconnaissance, plenty of staff work. Waterloo was a man of talent facing a man of genius, and mere talent won, I'm afraid.'

Out of the corner of my eye I can see Virginia yawning. I frown at her and she does an extra-big yawn and then looks sideways at me. I wonder if I can get away with sticking my tongue out, but decide maybe not yet.

'. . . rescued by bloody Blücher and his Prussians!' Hugh is saying, doubtless concluding some amusing anecdote.

I smile encouragingly at Hugh, who looks puzzled, so maybe it wasn't an amusing anecdote after all. I move quickly to a sympathetic frown and say: 'Quite so,' in what strikes me as an unfortunate and unintentional parody of Hugh's own style. Fortunately, nobody seems to have noticed this. Unfortunately, I still have no idea what Hugh was talking about.

'I think it's probably true,' I say, neatly sidestepping the

47

ranks of inconvenient, blue-coated Prussians, 'that mere talent usually wins over genius.'

Hugh looks genuinely interested. 'Does it?' he asks earnestly. 'Maybe you could give me some examples?'

'Marlborough . . .' I say, not being able to think of anyone else for the moment but keenly aware that I am already out of my depth.

'In which battle?' asks Hugh.

I try to remember whether it was Saxe that Marlborough fought against at Blenheim. If so, then hardly a genius . . .

'Or take Montgomery, for example,' I say, stumbling on blindly.

'That's *terribly* interesting,' he says.

I hear Virginia give a suppressed snigger in the background. I flash her a look of disapproval because, as I've said, I rather like Hugh and Daphne and I don't like Virginia mocking her father. Hopefully, Hugh did not hear the snigger.

'You may be right about Montgomery,' Hugh continues quickly. 'Rommel was by far the superior tactician. It would have been interesting to see what he could have done with the resources that Montgomery was given. Now, can I pour you some more of this Chablis? Then I've got a very good and rather unusual Meursault Rouge to follow, if you don't mind my saving your generous gift for another occasion. Don't worry about the Sussex police and their breathalysers. That daughter of mine, sniggering to herself over there on the far side of the table, can drive you back to London.'

* * *

But instead she has driven me to Worthing. I am not quite sure why, but after lunch she suggested heading down here for an hour or so, and we are now crunching along the beach, weaving an easy course between a few hardy souls who are absorbing the spring sunshine this evening. A damp breeze is drifting fitfully off the choppy, colourless sea and people are burrowing into bags to find jerseys and anoraks. Ahead of us, but still distant, two children are arguing on opposite sides of a complex sandcastle that must have required planning permission.

Virginia pauses in her progress towards Shoreham or Brighton or wherever we are heading. The wind blows her hair this way and that, but she does not seem to notice.

'Chris,' she says, 'Mum thinks Dad's got another, woman.'

I can think of a number of responses to this. 'Fair enough,' is the first one to spring to mind. What I actually say is: 'Surely not?'

'It happens,' she says, possibly thinking of her own Julian disaster.

'What exactly did she say to you?' I ask.

'Not a lot. She'd had a bit too much wine at lunch. When we were washing-up, she suddenly told me she'd found a strange letter to Hugh from a Woman.'

This, I should add, is another of the charming old-world customs that Virginia's parents maintain: after lunch, the girls wash up.

But still, a Woman.

'With a capital W?' I say.

'That was the way she described her.'

'And the strange letter said?'

'I don't know; it was something about their meeting up. That's as far as the discussion went, I'm afraid. Mum had equally sudden second thoughts, cancelling out the original ones. She said that maybe it didn't matter after all and passed me a saucepan to dry. It was the large one with string round the handle.'

'Maybe it doesn't matter,' I say.

Virginia shrugs.

We resume our walk, wondering whether it matters or whether it doesn't. It's a tricky one. Neither of us has as yet come to any conclusion. But the idea hangs there, like the mild pain in your chest that you ought to get checked out, but that is, quite possibly, just a mild pain in the chest. So for the moment we're ignoring it, but deep down I don't think this one is going away for good.

We are now closing in on the two sandcastle builders. They are in similar swimming trunks: one pair red, one pair green. The nearest child is a slightly taller version of the other. You do not have to be Mendel to work out that they are probably older and younger brother. The younger (green) version is around five. The older (red) one already looks a bit of a thug and proves it by taking a poorly aimed swing at his sibling just as we draw level. 'Well, *I* think it's a horrible castle,' he says, and he concludes what seems to have been a long and helpful discussion on the subject by stomping on a section of outer ramparts with his bare foot. It's an irrefutable argument, in my view; you have to admire him for that. I wait, however, to see whether the smaller one has the guts to kick him where it hurts. But he just snivels a bit. So my money's on the red one, if anyone's still taking bets.

'And tell *Mummy* if you want to,' sneers the odds-on favourite, expertly pre-empting any appeal to higher authority.

Game over, frankly. I am all for getting away from the scene of the crime before we might have to intervene like grown-ups, but Virginia is made of sterner stuff. 'Is that a nice thing to say?' she demands of the larger child.

'Yes,' he says after only the shortest consideration. He looks Virginia in the eye and then belches loudly – possibly a newly acquired skill. So much for grown-up intervention, then. He sprints away towards a distant family group, but not before lashing out with a toe and collapsing another tower into a heap of dry sand. Only the flapping red paper flag, now sticking out at forty-five degrees, gives a clue to its former glory. Time to go.

Virginia is on her knees beside the younger one in seconds. 'It's a lovely castle,' she says quickly. 'Did it take you a long time to build it?'

The child nods. He is not sure whether to cry, but if he does cry he's going to cry a lot. I remain very much in favour of moving on. Virginia puts an arm round his goose-pimpled shoulder.

'Can I help?' she asks. 'Can we make that tower again?'

The child nods again and sniffs, sucking back in an amber gobbet of snot that was attempting to escape from his nose. '*Handkerchief!*' I want to yell at him, but he is already absorbed, patting away at a little mound of sand, while

Virginia, kneeling in her favourite, dry-clean-only silk dress, fills one of the two buckets.

'Are you somebody's mummy?' he asks after a while, rubbing a layer of sand over the remaining snot.

'Not yet,' says Virginia, expertly patting out a tower and replanting the flag.

'Is he somebody's daddy?'

'Not as far as he knows,' says Virginia.

'He looks like a daddy.'

'Do you think so?' asks Virginia thoughtfully. 'I've sometimes wondered whether he could be turned into one.'

'He's got daddy hair,' says the child.

Meaning what exactly?

'Hmmm,' says Virginia, nodding.

Meaning *what* exactly?

I look towards the distant family group in the hope of seeing a parent striding our way, anxious to protect their child from the attention of dubious strangers. Nothing doing, unfortunately. It's just the three of us.

'Do you like making sandcastles?' asks the child, moving the conversation to a more interesting topic.

'Everyone likes making sandcastles,' says Virginia. 'Daddies like it most of all. Why don't we dig a moat here and then send Chris down to the sea with one of the buckets? We can make him run up and down the beach for us, carrying water. We can see if he is genuine daddy material. That would be funny, wouldn't it?'

'No,' I say.

'Yes,' says the child, cheering up, 'that would be *very* funny.' His grubby face looks up at me and his eyes meet mine with a steely, pale-blue gaze. He offers me the bright yellow bucket.

'Run, Daddy,' he says. 'Run.'

* * *

Sunday and it's raining. Virginia is at her work thing. I could check my emails. Equally, I think, as I switch my computer on, I could play Championship Manager for just a bit. I insert the CD-ROM and the game starts to run.

Championship Manager is not the most sophisticated computer game on the market, having been around a few years, but I like it. You get to manage a football team, you buy and sell players, you pick a team, work out tactics, hit the return key and wait for the computer to play the next match. It's a bit like following a real game on the BBC Sport website – you get updates on progress: the free kicks, the fouls, the cards, the GOALS. Then – and this is the bit that fascinates me – as your game ends, the computer gives you the results of all of the other matches that were being played that day. Somewhere, unknown to you, it has been running through match after match for all of the other teams – teams your team will never play and whose players you will never buy – and evaluating them, working out what the score should be. A whole invisible world of football is going on.

I call up a saved game that I've been playing for some time. We're several seasons ahead of real life. I am managing (Dave's) Southend United, in the hope of taking them up into the Premiership and onwards to the Champions' League. Unfortunately, as in real life, they have been relegated to the lower reaches of the football world.

It hurts. I almost got them into the Premiership a couple of seasons back, but missed the play-offs by one lousy point. My stupid computerized players screwed it up and, like remembering what you were doing when you heard about Kennedy being shot or whatever, I can recall every bit of the surrounding detail. There had been an earthquake somewhere like Pakistan, and Virginia had phoned me up just to ask whether I'd heard and to tell me how terrible it was that so many children had died. But all I could think was that I'd just missed promotion by *one lousy point*. Not having lost all grip on reality, I realized that I would be ill-advised to try to share my pain with Virginia, who might think that these children – whom I'd never seen and who I never knew existed before that day – were in some way more important than a computer game. But I can still remember the name of the player who scored the vital own goal (I sold him straight away) whereas I can't remember for certain if the earthquake was in Pakistan or some other place entirely.

Outside, the rain is now coming down in a steady stream but the computer tells me that it's fine and pitch conditions are good for the next match. I'm not planning to go out this morning. So which weather is more real? Eh?

* * *

I dodge quickly out of Great Portland Street station, but in the fairly safe knowledge that none of my staff will be abroad at this hour. It is still eight thirty and I need to catch Humph, who was away again most of last week, to discuss two matters of great importance before the Society office gets too busy.

Humph is already at his desk as expected. Possibly he really does have no home to go to. Today there are dark rings under his eyes and he looks not so much tired as ill – 'gaunt' would describe it best, but 'ashen' isn't a bad description either. The shirt, however, is crisp and white and the suit is soft and blue, and his shoes shine brightly, so all is not lost. He also retains his slightly patrician air. The President told me a story about Humph last week. He'd proposed that Humph's title should be changed from Secretary to Chief Executive, and thought Humph might be pleased. Humph had pondered this for no more than a second before replying: 'Secretary is an old and honourable title. Royal societies such as ours have had Secretaries since the seventeenth century at least. I would not recommend precipitous change.' The President, who is not that tall, had drawn himself up to his full height to imitate Humph delivering this final rebuke. 'I would not,' he repeated with a frown, 'recommend precipitous change.' Classic Humph, really.

'Have you got a couple of minutes?' I ask Humph.

He waves a hand noncommittally, inviting me over the threshold and into his office, but he does not ask me to sit. 'Chris,' he once said to me, 'remember this: if you don't want somebody to stay, don't ask then to sit.' Actually, he's said it several times. I can't stand it when people keep repeating the same old lines over and over.

'I put George Magwitch in touch with a journalist,' I say.

'Somebody dull? Somebody reliable?'

'Absolutely.'

'Then pray do not tell me who it is. I know as much as is good for me.'

'Do you? Right. If you say so. One other thing, though.'

'Yes?' Humph rubs his eyes, but the dark rings aren't going to go away that easily.

'When are you going to advertise the Deputy post?' I ask.

'Ah,' he says, glumly. 'Perhaps you'd better sit down.'

I sit, wondering what is in store. He's about to do more than just give me a date for my diary. He's going to give me bad news. Somebody has just whipped my stomach out and replaced it with a lump of cold jelly. I hate it when they do that.

'We're going to offer the post to Brindley,' he says.

'Poxy Passmore? Just like that? No advert? No interviews?'

'Yes, just like that,' he says.

'Can you do that? Is it legal? Can I appeal?'

'I've done it. You can appeal if you like, but I wouldn't. You don't want the job, Chris.'

'Don't I?' This is news to me.

'The Deputy post ain't worth a pitcher of warm piss,' he drawls in an American accent. It's another one of his quotes, and I'm expected to recognize it, which maybe I do, but I'm not going to give him the satisfaction. He raises a mildly disappointed eyebrow at my lack of reaction, then continues: 'We decided not to advertise it because it's only Brindley's current job with a new fancy title – managing the accounts, the building, IT, HR, catering. OK, it's bit more than that – he takes over Membership Department and CPD – and he *will* deputize for me if I'm on leave – or sick – but it's all the boring bits of the Society, when it comes down to it. You can do better than that.'

'Can I?' I hope he catches the note of irony, which is definitely there. I think I'd be pretty good managing HR, actually. Maybe not IT.

'Look, Chris, nobody knows this yet, but I'm likely to retire a year or two earlier than I had planned.'

'Why?'

Humph waves a hand limply. 'I'll tell all of you in good time.'

I look again at the grey face, the bags under the eyes. I'm glad I don't look like that. What am I supposed to say? How long have you got to live?

'How . . . soon are you planning to leave?' is what I find I've actually said.

'Later this year,' says Humph. 'I don't know exactly. But when I do go I want you to apply for my job.'

'Me?' I say.

'Don't sound so surprised. You've been here a while. Anyway, it's time you took on some serious responsibility.'

'I thought I had a responsible job.'

'Very. For somebody in their mid-twenties. How old are you?'

'What's that got to do with anything?' I ask.

'You try to dress as if you were still a nineteen-year-old student.'

I check out what I am wearing – new leather jacket, pure white Ralph Lauren Purple Label T-shirt, pristine Levi's, Tod's loafers. Student? I somehow doubt that a student could afford *this* jacket.

'What's wrong with the way I dress?'

'Nothing at all, if you don't want people to take you seriously. Socks would be a good start.'

Well, I don't want to dress like you either, I think. At least I look vaguely as if I belong to the twenty-first century.

'And then there are the new terms of reference for the Ethics and Rights Committee,' says Humph wearily.

'You've read them?'

'Why did you include a requirement that all committee members should have beards?'

'Did I leave that in? It was only a joke. I thought I'd deleted it.'

'No, you didn't, though I now have. I'm not suggesting that you shouldn't have fun, Chris, but you clearly can't be bothered to check things and you don't seem to realize that your humour is sometimes badly misplaced.'

'Sorry.'

'You're a grown-up now, Chris,' Humph continues. 'You have reached the age of reason, as somebody once described it.'

Another quote I am supposed to recognize, clearly. Shall I tell him I know it's Sartre? No, I can't be arsed.

'Chris,' says Humph, 'what *is* your problem?'

'I'll get a suit,' I say.

'You know that's not what I mean,' says Humph.

'It's a start, though, isn't it?' I say.

He stands up. The interview is over. Depart in peace.

I close his door as I leave. I figure he can do with a bit of quiet.

So there you are. Humph's dying. I'm going to get his job.

And it's still only eight forty-five on Monday morning. It could be quite a week.

* * *

'OK, boys and girls, let's kick the week off,' I say.

The 'Team' are sitting round in a circle, giving me their full attention. Narinder is leaning forward in his chair, black, slightly greasy hair flopping into his eyes, looking keen and alert. Jon is (conversely) leaning back, hands behind his head, his face showing no more than mild curiosity. Fatima is frowning and fiddling with a notebook, which refuses to sit flat on her lap. Lucy is wearing another tight sweater – pale blue cashmere today – and a very short black skirt. She smiles at me. I smile back. It's a shame that the one big piece of news I've had today is something I can't tell them.

'I'm going to be sending you an email on annual leave allocations later today . . .' I begin.

'You sent us half an email on Friday,' says Jon with a grin.

'I think you pressed SEND when you meant to press SAVE,' says Narinder earnestly.

'Whatever,' I say. 'These things happen. I'll finish it and send it again. OK, Jon, tell us just how dull the next five days are going to be for *you*.'

Jon stretches and straightens, and then he says: 'Things are back to normal now that I no longer have Digby Spain chasing me. God, that man's evil. Anyway, I managed to do a lot of work on the press database last week, and I should finish inputting this week, unless a real PR crisis hits us.'

I am trying to work out whether Lucy can possibly be wearing a bra under that sweater and am just saying, 'Thanks, Jon. Over to you, Narinder,' when an alarm bell starts to ring deafeningly and I have to stop and interject: '*Digby Spain?*'

'Yes, I told you last week,' says Jon.

'Remind me,' I say.

'I didn't think you were listening,' says Jon. He leans back in his chair again and grins. He is a very happy bunny all of a sudden.

I am not. 'Cut the crap, Jon. Just remind me.'

'I told you that Mr Spain had been pestering me for information on our Professor Magwitch.'

I've probably mentioned that I hate it when they do that cold-jelly-for-stomach exchange thing?

'What was he after?' I also hate it when they swap your tongue for one three sizes too big.

'Don't worry. I gave nothing away at all. I'd already been tipped off that he was a friend of Dan Smith's lawyer. Now Smith's been cleared, he's gunning for Magwitch as the chief prosecution witness. Smith's supporters claim Magwitch's evidence was inaccurate, biased and unprofessional and they want him to – quote – suffer as Dan Smith had to suffer – unquote.'

'A friend of Dan Smith's lawyer?' I say. This is not good news.

'Apparently. Anyway, I spent a whole week fending Spain off, but it all went quiet after last Monday for some reason. He's got no idea how to get hold of Magwitch, so there's not a lot he can do.' Jon folds his arms, pleased that he has handled this well, and that I, in his place, might have made a mess of it. What he doesn't know, of course, is that I have made a mess of it anyway.

'Why didn't you tell me any of this?' I demand.

'I did. I told you all of it last Monday. You really weren't listening, were you? I suspect your mind may have been elsewhere.' His eyes move imperceptibly but significantly towards Lucy. Has anyone except me noticed? Jon smiles a relaxed smile. 'Anyway, why worry? No harm done. Digby's stuffed.'

'Look,' I say to the Team, trying not to let my voice switch from baritone to soprano, as it strangely wishes to do. 'I've just realized that there's something I need to sort out urgently. We'll have to finish here.'

Narinder looks hurt. 'But, man, I've got lots to tell the team about my week.'

'Save it,' I say. 'Surprise us next week.'

Narinder exchanges a puzzled glance with Lucy. Jon is still grinning, even though he's got no idea just how much he's got to grin about, and Fatima is still trying to get her notebook flat. She looks up suddenly, because she too has not been fully attending up to this point. 'So, do you want me to write up the minutes?' she asks testily.

'Let's leave Chris to it,' says Lucy, ushering them all out, like the school monitor she so recently might have been. If I had not been so concerned about other things I might have worried about the rather proprietorial manner she is developing towards me. But for the moment I scarcely register it. 'Let me know if any of us can help,' she adds as she closes the door.

I immediately phone George Magwitch and he immediately answers.

'Did you speak to Digby Spain?' I demand, without any of the usual polite preliminaries, like 'hello'. I hope he'll say something reassuring like: 'No, I was diagnosed with leprosy and decided not to bother,' but he just grunts affirmatively. A picture of a happy pig flashes briefly in front of me: a pig who hasn't yet heard about bacon slicers.

'Yes, I phoned him straight away,' says the temporarily happy pig. 'We had a long chat. A very long chat.'

'And?'

'And he's gone away to talk to other people and write it up.'

'Other people?' I enquire nervously. 'What type of other people?'

'I didn't think to ask. People who would back up my side of the story, I guess,' says the Happy Pig.

'And how was he generally?' I ask, hoping that there may be some microscopic straw to clutch at.

'In rude health, I would imagine. No coughs or sniffles over the phone anyway. I didn't take a full medical history.'

'No,' I say, in the slow and clear way you do when speaking to an idiot. 'Was he friendly?'

'Funny you should ask that. I found him a bit more distant than you led me to believe he might be. Once or twice I had to remind him to call me George rather than Professor Magwitch. But he was very polite. Very proper. Say what you like about journalists *qua* journalists, but Digby's a real gent. I imagine he went to the right sort of school. I must ask him where.'

'What did you *tell* him?'

'Well, since he's a mate of yours, Chris, pretty much everything. I certainly left him in no doubt about Dan Smith.'

'Precisely what did you say?' I have my fingers crossed on both hands, but it's not as reliable a method of avoiding disaster as you would think.

'Well, low IQ, no qualifications, only working because he's not bright enough to be a benefit fraudster, almost certainly been a bully all his life. Probably an Arsenal supporter.'

'I'm an Arsenal supporter,' I point out.

'There you are then,' George says cheerfully. 'He seemed proud to have had parents who beat him within an inch of his life when he was a kid – thought a quick slap was the solution to most problems. A wife beater too, I would think. Should never have been allowed near a care home, let alone permitted to work unsupervised for long periods.'

Excellent.

'Benefit fraudster? Wife beater? Did you actually *say* any of that? Please tell me that you didn't.' I'm pretty sure I know the answer, but it's worth asking the question.

There is a low chuckle down the line. 'Maybe. I really can't remember now. If it helps, I definitely didn't say he was an Arsenal supporter. I also explained carefully how the medical evidence had stacked up. Anyway, Spain's a friend, isn't he? He won't quote things that I obviously intended to be off the record. He's hardly likely to stitch you up, is he?'

Of course, George Magwitch is right. Theoretically, there

is always a chance that Digby Spain is not going to stitch me up. Because there is a theoretical chance of even the most unlikely things.

5

Neuburg, Danube Valley, November 1619

The waiter wiped his sleeve across his nose and knocked on the door. 'Breakfast!' he announced. The door swung open and a bearded face looked down at him.

'Breakfast, good sir,' said the waiter cheerfully, ever mindful of the fact that there was still a chance of a tip. 'Chicken and our fine white bread.'

'Is it as bad as last night's supper?' asked Descartes.

The waiter pondered. 'What did you have for supper?'

'Beef.'

'No, it's not as bad as that,' he conceded.

He crossed the room and set the platter of chicken and bread down on the table.

'How's the old philosophy going, then?' the waiter asked conversationally. 'Now that I'm a philosopher myself, I have a professional interest.'

'I've just proved the existence of God,' said Descartes.

'That's nice,' said the waiter, setting a knife down by the

food and arranging a cleanish napkin on the other side. 'Would you like beer with that?'

'Don't you want to know how?'

'I suppose it could come in useful,' said the waiter. 'Is it quick, or should I take a seat?

'Take a seat. Now, yesterday we had reached a point where we doubted everything except our own existence.'

The waiter put his hand up.

'Yes?' sighed Descartes, knowing that intelligent questions at this point were not likely.

'We didn't doubt doubt,' said the waiter.

'That's what I mean,' said Descartes.

'Do you? Carry on then,' said the waiter magnanimously.

'But there are some things, even then, about which we can have some certainty.'

'H—' began the waiter.

'No, not sodding ham,' snapped Descartes. He paused for a moment, took a deep breath and continued, enunciating every word carefully. 'Let us consider a triangle. Even if I doubt the reality of material objects, it must be true that, defining a triangle as lines joining three points in space, the triangle must have three sides and three angles.'

'That's why it's called a triangle,' said the waiter helpfully.

'Indeed,' said Descartes. 'And I do not need to see a physical triangle to know that its internal angles will add up to one hundred and eighty degrees.'

'And that's true of squares?'

'Yes, except it's three hundred and sixty degrees, obviously.'

'And pentagons?'

'Yes. Except it's five hundred and forty degrees.'

'And hexagons.'

'Yes.'

'And—'

'Yes, yes, yes – before we have to consider sixty-seven-sided polygons – yes, *all* geometrical figures. It is easier to be certain about abstractions than it is about physical objects.'

'I don't know what an abstraction is,' said the waiter.

'You are very fortunate,' said Descartes. 'Just think of it as . . . an idea. Even with physical objects, however, it is possible to imagine only things that are based on what we have ourselves seen.'

'That's not true,' said the waiter.

'All right, imagine something that is totally unlike anything you have seen.'

'Very well, I am imagining a monster with claws like a lion, legs like a bull, a body like a sheep and a head like . . . like . . . another lion. I've never seen that. Not in Neuburg anyway.'

'But you have seen a lion and a sheep and a bull.'

'Granted.' The waiter gave the matter further thought. 'What about a monster with a body like a sheep and a head like a dragon and a beer gut like the cook's? I've never seen a dragon.'

'And what is a dragon like?'

'It's like a big lizard,' said the waiter, realizing at once that he had been caught in some sort of philosopher trap. 'Yes, I agree, I *have* seen a lizard.'

'Now consider me,' said Descartes. 'I am imperfect.'

'I wouldn't say that,' said the waiter, unwilling to offend a guest who might still wish to show his appreciation of good service.

'I must be imperfect, because I have doubts. But nevertheless, I can imagine perfection, as an abstraction. Perfection must therefore exist. But since my finite mind cannot conceive this infinite thing, it must exist outside me. And this perfection we call . . .'

'God?'

'Exactly.'

'But that only proves he might exist.'

'No, it proves he does exist. If we define God as a perfect being, then a perfect being must have the property of existence, or he would not be perfect.'

'And that's it? The proof? All of it?'

'More or less. I need to work on it a bit, obviously.'

'And is that the end of the argument?'

'No,' said Descartes. 'Clearly a perfect God would not deceive me about reality. So I need not doubt my senses any longer.'

'You wouldn't call that argument a bit circular – your certainty that God exists depending, as it does, on God's assurance to you that your senses don't deceive you?'

'No.'

The waiter got to his feet. 'Good – so we both exist. Well, I'm glad we've cleared that one up, then. That leaves you free to eat and me to serve you. Did you say you wanted a tankard of beer or not?'

'Is it as bad as the wine?'

'Did the wine keep you up all night with the shits?'

'No.'

'I'd stick to the wine then.'

'I hope you realize,' said Descartes, as the waiter turned to go, 'that you have been present at one of the turning points of western philosophy?'

The waiter closed the door carefully. 'I doubt that,' he said.

6

No Date

It is not uncommon to lose one's belief in God. At what point, I wonder, did I lose my belief in reality?

It can't have happened suddenly. These things don't, do they? No fiery writing in the sky: 'It's all in your imagination, Chris.' No unexpected text message from the Holy Ghost. Just a growing sense of unease.

Had I lived a hundred years ago, I might have struggled to reconcile a benign deity and a world in which children starved to death before they were a year old. I might have wondered about God's Purpose. I might have concluded that God at least knew what was going on and he would let me in on the joke when he thought fit. But since I was born into the second half of the twentieth century, as part of the first generation to understand the term 'virtual reality', my view of life was necessarily different. If this world did not make sense on its own, then surely it was because we were seeing only part of the picture. And the other half of the picture did not need to be God. The 'reality' that we experience could have been produced by any programmer with the right software and a broadband connection. It was true that nobody *within this reality* had the skills or the kit, but which was more likely: software slightly more powerful than the PlayStation, or an omnipotent, omnipresent God, virgin birth, water turned into wine and so on and so on? No contest.

I started wandering round the streets looking at people and thinking: 'Yes, very lifelike, but do you exist? Had one of them answered my unspoken thoughts by turning and replying: 'Of course I do, Chris,' then I would have been onto their game like a shot. But they simply passed by on their programmed course, giving nothing away.

Then, other days – most days really – I would think: No, maybe it's real after all. Maybe there's no God and no other reality beyond this one. Maybe this is it. Maybe we just *are*.

I really needed to discuss this with somebody – preferably somebody that I was reasonably certain existed. I tried talking to Dave about it one evening but he just said . . .

7

Another Pub, 27 April this Year

'. . . Sorry, Chris, that's a bit too hypothetical to take in at this stage in the evening.'

We are sitting in a pub just off Great Portland Street. He's been there a bit longer than I have and so is slightly less capable of rational thought.

'But Descartes doubted reality,' I say.

'No,' says Dave, prodding my chest with a damp beer-mat, 'Descartes postulated that our senses might deceive us, but only as a step towards proving that they did not.' For a fat drunken slob, Dave knows quite a lot about philosophy. He really does. Dave claims, in fact, to have a degree in philosophy, but he's never said how many cornflake-packet tops he had to send in to get it.

'What about Berkeley?' I say.

'Berkeley questions whether a tree falling in an uninhabited forest, with nobody to hear it fall, makes a noise. He did not refute the authenticity of our existence.'

'What about *The Matrix*?'

'It's a film,' says the holder of a genuine degree in philosophy. 'I missed most of it because the activities of the couple in the row in front of me were much more entertaining. *Groundhog Day*, in my view, raises far more complex questions about the nature of reality. Whose round is it?'

'Yours,' I say.

Instead of springing to his podgy little legs and fetching me a nice cold Tiger, Dave sits there for a bit, looking at me, and then says: 'How's Virginia?'

'OK,' I say cautiously.

'How's Lucy?'

'OK,' I say again. If Dave is trying to take this anywhere, I'm not planning to help him on his way.

'You really need to sort your life out,' he says.

'No,' I say. 'No, Dave, I do not need to sort my life out, because my life is fine, thank you very much.'

'And Virginia's life?'

'I've no complaints.'

'That's not what I meant either.'

'Sorry, David, what is your point *exactly*?'

'I think Virginia deserves better. One day you're off to Brighton with her – the next you're snuggling down with Lucy to watch old videos . . .'

'Lucy didn't show up,' I say. I hadn't been planning to tell Dave this, of course. 'So nobody snuggled down with anyone. I hate to disappoint you but I spent Thursday night with a good book. There was some mix-up over dates. We're going to do it some other time.'

'Then sort yourself out before you do.'

'Do you know?' I say. 'You're getting old and boring. It's the same thing all the time.'

'Like your jokes,' he says. 'Confucius he say: "I tell joke once, you laugh, joke good. I tell same joke second time, you laugh, joke *very* good. I tell joke third time, you laugh, you moron."'

Like I say, Dave's a red-hot philosopher.

I left the pub early, and not just because it was my round.

It was raining slightly: the sort of gentle and persistent drizzle that makes you feel stupid wandering around with an umbrella, but which makes you feel damp if you don't. I should never have started the discussion with Dave about reality. It just reminds me about . . . well, stuff in general. Nothing I've got plans to tell you or anyone else about.

It was starting to get dark. The shops had closed, apart from the small newsagents that you get all over London, selling papers and sweets and booze and ibuprofen twenty-four hours a day. Inside the restaurants the lights were on and, if you slowed down a little as you passed, you could see the people inside, seated in twos and threes and fours, ordering their food, sipping their wine with a thoughtful air, talking, happy. If all of this existed only in my mind, then each little scene had been constructed with great care – the diners, the waiters, the menus – all put there just so that I could view them briefly as I passed by. A bus drew up close by, sucked in a gaggle of passengers from the bus stop, and headed off towards South London. Or so it claimed on the illuminated sign on the front. Obviously, once out of my sight, it could just have vanished in a puff of smoke, to re-emerge only when I needed to be conscious of it again.

The rain was falling heavily and just a bit too realistically.

I turned up my coat collar and quickened my pace towards the tube station.

Dave was presumably still sitting comfortably in the pub, finishing his beer. Of course, he was right in a way about Virginia and Lucy. I did need to do something about them. Assuming that they all exist, of course.

Assuming that any one of them exists.

* * *

I've been back in my flat for about fifteen minutes when the phone rings. It's Virginia's father.

'Chris?' he says. 'Hugh here.'

I confirm my identity (name, rank and number – ha, ha) and ask what I can do for him.

'It's the Minden regiments piece,' he says. 'I was wondering whether to concentrate on the battle or on the regiments themselves. I'd like your advice.'

I give him my views and also a possibly useful reference in Robert Graves' *Goodbye to All That* about continuing links between the regiments.

He thanks me and, for a moment, I wonder if he has just phoned up to flatter me that I genuinely know something he doesn't – to make me feel better about myself. It is the sort of thing that Hugh would do. The memory of Virginia kneeling in the sand, helping reconstruct the sandcastle, suddenly comes back to me. There's a link between these two unrelated events, an invisible thread that joins it all together.

The other thought that comes back to me is that Virginia's

mother thinks he has a Woman stashed away somewhere. If so, good for Hugh, but I doubt it somehow.

'If I think of anything else, I'll let you know,' I say.

'Thanks,' he says.

Then the subject of conversation does a quick left turn. 'Did you see Virginia yesterday?' he asks in an oddly detached way.

'No,' I say, 'she was at that work thing,' Doesn't she tell her father anything? Then, for the first time, it strikes me that I really know nothing at all about the 'work thing' either. That is the only description Virginia has ever given me of it. I haven't bothered to ask for details.

'It's just . . .' he begins. There is a pause during which I can hear him thinking, 'I don't want to worry you in the slightest,' because that's the sort of thing that Hugh thinks all the time, bless him. 'It's just that she usually phones us on Sunday evening and she didn't. I can't get her this evening either and wondered if maybe she was with you.'

'No, she's not here,' I say, not worried.

'She's always working late,' he says.

'We all do,' I say. 'That's how things are these days.'

'Not for me.' He chuckles. 'Not since I retired. You should try it. In the meantime, don't work too hard, and thanks again for the advice on Royal Welch Fusiliers.'

'Happy birthday for tomorrow,' I say.

We hang up – I in Islington and he in Horsham – and go about our business. I check my copy of *Goodbye to All That* and find I have completely misremembered the quote, which is actually about another battle entirely. For a moment I consider phoning Hugh back but then I realize that he's not

76

planning to use the quote anyway. The call was about Virginia. He's worried and there's something he's being careful not to tell me. And this is odd because, apart from the odd fancy woman, Hugh has no secrets from anyone. Not from me, not from Virginia. None at all.

* * *

I've got an important meeting at the Society today; so I am smartly dressed in my new leather jacket, simple but very expensive white T-shirt, classic jeans and Tod's loafers. No socks.

But, first, I need to catch Jon.

'Jon,' I say, 'this Digby Spain thing . . .'

'Nothing to worry about, Chris,' he says. 'No contact with him for ages.'

'But what do you think he was trying to get out of you?'

'Just George Magwitch's contact details.'

'And you think he's going to stitch me – Magwitch, that is – up.'

Jon is looking at me oddly. 'Is there something I need to know?' he asks.

'No,' I say, giving him the reassuring smile, 'I just wanted to make sure we were both saying the same thing if he tried again.'

'He won't contact you. He knows that I deal with the press.'

'I dealt with him over the faked research.'

'Yes,' says Jon, 'but that was a while ago, before I arrived. I deal with the press now. With respect, the last thing

I need is you or somebody else here trying to do my job for me. It's fine as it is.'

'Maybe I should give him a call though?'

'No,' says Jon. 'That's the one thing you should not do.'

* * *

'Spain,' says a bored voice.

'Hi, Digby, my old friend. Chris here,' I say. 'How's tricks?'

'Chris?'

'Chris Sorensen.'

'Ah, Christian . . . yes, of course, how can I help you?'

'I just wondered how your chat with George had gone.'

'Professor Magwitch? Fine. Thank you very much for arranging it. I am eternally grateful.'

'I just need to check what George told you.'

'He told me what I needed to know.'

'Which was?'

'His side of the story.'

Not giving much away then, our Digby. I try a pre-emptive strike.

'Look,' I say, in my most honeyed tones, 'old George can be fairly outspoken. That's why they like having him as a panellist on *Question Time* – you know how he likes to wind people up. He can say some pretty stupid things. A lot of his colleagues hate his guts for obvious reasons. I mean, he's not exactly politically correct, is he? But, Digby, he's a decent sort of guy. That's the real story. He's the sort of doctor they don't make any more. A man of principle and integrity. Plenty of people care about kids. He cares about everyone.

Think of him as a Cumbrian Mother Teresa. Do you know how many lives he has saved? Do you?'

'No, he didn't say. How many? It would be useful to have that.'

I realize that I actually don't know either, so I quickly say: 'So, you mustn't take his views about Dan Smith too seriously.'

'Which views?'

'About his being a wife beater or a benefit cheat.'

'I don't think he said either of those things. Is that his view then? He thinks Dan Smith is a benefit cheat?'

'No,' I say. 'Not at all.' I say it fast, but there is of course no way that I can say it quite fast enough at this stage.

'So,' says Digby, like somebody with all the time in the world, 'let me get this right – were *you* calling him a benefit cheat then?'

'No.'

'I'm sure I heard somebody say it,' says Digby Spain with what can only be described as mock-puzzlement. Smug git. 'Now, you said that Professor Magwitch often said stupid things. What did you mean by that?'

'I didn't say that exactly.'

There is a pause. 'According to my notes, you did.'

'Are you taking *notes*?' I say, out of more than mild curiosity.

'I always take notes. You'd be surprised how easy it is to forget things if you don't.'

This is true. I try to remember, not having taken notes myself, exactly what I've said so far. Did I, for example, imply that George Magwitch was the last remaining doctor on the planet with any sort of integrity? That may not play too well with doctors generally, such as our President, our Vice-Presidents, our chairs of committees and indeed the entire paying membership of the Society. So it may be better if Digby doesn't quote me on that either.

'Obviously this is off the record,' I suggest. Even to myself, I do not sound that confident.

'In what sense do you mean: *obviously*?' Digby enquires. I think he may be smiling, but possibly not in a good way.

'Press Office briefings usually are.'

'Not in my experience. In any case, Jon is your press man, isn't he?'

I wonder if it would be possible to rewind this conversation back to the beginning and start all over again, either with me not making the phone call at all or possibly introducing myself as 'Narinder'.

'So, why do Professor Magwitch's colleagues hate him?' asks Digby.

'Did I say that?' *Did* I say that?

'Well, you actually said that they hated his guts, but I take it they hate the rest of him as well.' Digby's enjoying this.

'That was definitely off the record,' I say.

'Christian, could I give you some advice?'

'Of course, Digby, of course.' Is he offering me a lifeline?

'If you want something to be off the record, tell the journalist before you open your big mouth. Or better still, don't open it at all.' Well, that's cleared that one up: he's not offering me a lifeline.

'If you write that George Magwitch is hated by his colleagues, I'll deny ever having said anything of the sort.'

'I'm sure you will,' says Digby genially. 'It has the ring of truth, though. I can see why he would be a rather abrasive and difficult colleague. Thanks, Christian. That is very insightful.'

Even I can see this is not going well. Of course, that doesn't mean I can't make things worse.

'Look, Digby, you'll treat this whole conversation as off the record or there'll be trouble,' I say.

Digby Spain is laughing so much that there is, I am delighted to say, a genuine chance he will choke to death. 'Can I quote you on that?' he asks.

* * *

I check my mail and immediately call Jon into my office.

'What's this new email from Passmore?' I say, once he has closed the door.

'The one about staff relationships?' he says. Like Digby Spain, he's smiling.

'Yes,' I say. Or possibly I hiss it. My voice is doing all sorts of things this morning without checking with my brain first. Maybe after the Digby Spain conversation it reckons it's safer making the decisions on its own.

'The email's nothing new,' says Jon, 'just a reminder about what it says in the Staff Handbook. Senior staff are not supposed to have close personal relationships – and absolutely zero sexual relationships – with staff working for them. You and Lucy, for example.' Jon is smirking from ear to ear as he says this last bit.

'What business is it of bloody Passmore's?' I demand.

'Technically, none at all. You will see that he has signed himself Deputy Secretary – a promotion as yet unannounced. Roger will not be too pleased about that. I fear, however, that this is the shape of things to come. We'll be seeing a lot of these little edicts once Brindley Passmore really gets his feet under the table as deputy führer.'

'And it's aimed at me?'

'And Lucy,' he says. 'But mainly at you.'

'How does he know about that?'

'The two of you have been a bit obvious, don't you think? You might try going off to lunch at slightly different times. Also I can't remember when I last had a three-hour discussion with you with the door closed.'

'The door's closed now. I am nevertheless not ravishing you on Society premises. Nor do I plan to.'

'I'm not a twenty-two-year-old girl wearing a purely token attempt at a skirt.'

'We're just friends,' I say.

'I know,' he says. 'I have never imagined for a moment that there was anything going on at all. I mean, you and Lucy . . .' His smile dismisses the very idea of it.

I am a bit put out that he is so certain but I just say: 'There you are, then.'

'You're much too old for her.'

'Thanks.' I do my best to make it sound as if I am joking, but am aware that I may not have entirely succeeded. Anyway, I scarcely think Jon is in a position to accuse anyone of being too old.

'What I don't understand,' he says, 'is why you both seem

to be doing everything possible to confirm everyone's worst suspicions.'

'Like I say – it's our business.'

There is a nominal knock on the door and Susan, the Society's Archivist and thus one of Passmore's myrmidons, is suddenly in our midst, clutching a bundle of papers to her chest. She is dressed entirely in black as usual. Her red lipstick (Clinique – Current Plum) is the one flash of colour.

'I hope I'm not interrupting anything important?' she enquires sweetly. I wonder how much of the conversation she has already heard.

Jon is now looking out of the window so it's down to me to grade the importance of the discussion we have been having.

'As you are aware, Susan, I don't *do* anything important,' I say. '*E fortiori* our middle-aged colleague on my left.'

'Do you know? That's exactly what Brindley tells everyone,' she says, looking from Jon to me and then back again. 'I'll go away and let you get on with your inconsequential conversation then, but first I need to check if you have a copy of the June 1998 Society Newsletter; Brindley thought you might, and I need one to complete the run in the archives.'

'I'll see if I've got one and send it over later,' I say. Then I add: 'Were you listening outside the door a moment ago?'

Susan flutters her mascaraed eyelashes (Maybelline – Sky-High Curves). 'Of course not,' she says with slightly too much sincerity. 'And in any case, I have no interest in your lunchtime arrangements, Chris. Unless you want to invite me, of course. Brindley wondered, by the way, what you thought of the new Staff Suggestion Box.'

'What's that?'

'All staff are being invited to make suggestions for improving the efficiency of their departments. He thought all of you in External Relations would have masses of ways of being more efficient.'

I decide not to rise to this one and just return her smile.

'By the way, he's thinking of introducing a dress code,' she adds. 'Suits and ties for all senior staff. Oh, and socks, I think, Chris.'

'Very amusing,' I say.

It's her turn to smile. I wonder if Passmore really thinks he can introduce a dress code in a twenty-first-century office. It's the sort of thing he'd try to do.

'Well, I'll leave you boys to it, then,' Susan says. 'Have a nice lunch, Chris. You and whoever the lucky girl is.'

'You see,' says Jon, after she has gone, 'it's obviously reached Brindley's people. Even if nothing is going on, everyone seems to have heard about it.'

'Stuff everyone,' I say.

'All the same, I wouldn't annoy him,' says Jon, in his capacity as the Oracle of Delphi.

I am well aware what happens to people who disrespect the Oracles. 'I'll annoy Brindley Passmore every bit as much as I want to,' I say. 'It's my right.'

Even on days when I choose to believe in the material existence of most of the universe I shall, I decide, always find room to make an exception for Poxy Passmore.

Though my office lies on the highly prestigious first floor and though I am only one degree removed from the very biggest cheeses of the Society, I take my turn in minuting committee meetings. Even Humph condescends to act as secretary to some exalted Society board. It's part of the job round here.

Today is the External Affairs Committee, which was set up at some time in the past to allow one Vice-President to score off another Vice-President, and which continues to function because nobody has found a way to disband it. It overlaps with, and badly hinders, many other Society committees; but that was precisely what it was created to do. It is fit for purpose.

My standard black and red A5 notebook is open in front of me. Occasionally I write something. Occasionally I look around the table. Occasionally I nod to the Chairman to show that I am awake and have noted some point on which action will need to be taken. Sometimes my views are sought, though often they are not.

I scribble a couple of words on the lined page and then re-read the notes that I have already made. So far, I have written this:

> As desert sands roll on, where nothing lives,
> And, grain on sterile grain, rise up in dunes,
> As lifeless water plays across the stones
> And painted flow'rs in frames seek to deceive,
> As marvels of the taxidermist's art
> Spring sightless, tongue-less from the plaster bough,
> With wings outstretched but stiff and useless now,

Dry bones, dry skin, dry talons, all inert;
Thus is the deadness of these living hours
These barren days, these barren months, these years
That drain our strength, our youth, our very powers
And bring the silent stones themselves to tears.
Where little's done and nothing's done in haste:
All time spent in committees is misplaced.

Well, it's a sonnet, right enough. No doubt about that. Not exactly Petrarchan and not exactly Shakespearian and not exactly a hybrid of the two. ABBA CDDC EFEFDD. It is, I decide, a Sorensenian sonnet, and eminently permissible. I have to admire my daring in rhyming not only 'stones' with 'dunes' but also 'lives' with 'deceive' (awesome) in the very same quatrain. Eat your heart out, Spenser. But 'powers' is frankly only in there for the rhyme, and I'm still not sure about that final couplet. I'd like to get the word 'waste' into it. In which case, maybe I could change the last line to . . .

'Did you get that action point, Chris?' asks the chairman, from a long way away.

'Absolutely,' I say, with a quick and confident smile.

And we move on to the next item on the agenda.

* * *

I dial Virginia's office number.

'Hi,' I say.

'Hello, darling,' she says. 'Is it important, because I'm just off to a meeting?'

'No, I just haven't heard from you for a day or two. Your

86

father called last night. We both wondered what you were up to.'

'Did you both? How sweet. I must ring Daddy this evening anyway. Thanks for the reminder.'

'How did your work thing go?'

'Work thing?'

'At the weekend.'

'Oh, that. Fine.'

'What was it exactly?'

'Oh, just people from work, getting together. Doing things.'

'Yes, I'd gathered that much.'

'Sorry, darling. I'd tell you if I thought you were interested, but honestly you're not. Grown-ups' stuff. Got to dash now. Love you!'

'Love you,' I say. But the line has already gone dead.

* * *

I dial Dave's work number.

'Hi,' I say.

'Chris,' he says. 'Haven't spoken to you since . . . last night. What can I do for you, mate?'

'Fancy a drink after work?' I ask.

'Sorry, mate,' says Dave. 'Not tonight. I'm taking Megan to see the new Johnny Depp picture.'

'Megan? Paul's Megan?'

'Megan,' he says. 'Just Megan.'

'I could come too,' I say, 'I haven't seen that one.'

'We're going straight after work,' he says.

I don't see how that rules me out, but I can see that he

might not want to expose Megan to competition like me. I point this out to him.

'Take Virginia to see it,' he says.

'OK,' I say. 'We'll do the drink tomorrow night.'

'Not sure what I'm doing tomorrow. I'll definitely catch up with you later this week. Sorry, Chris, I've got to dash.'

Where, I wonder, is everyone dashing to this morning? It's the pace of modern life, I guess. Soon they'll all be having nervous breakdowns.

* * *

I dial Lucy's work number and listen to the phone ring just outside my office door.

'Hi,' I say.

'Chris? I'm right here. Why are you phoning me?'

'Can't be arsed to open the door,' I say.

I hear her giggling without the aid of the phone.

'You can be so childish at times,' she says.

'Lunch, Villandry,' I say. 'I leave at twelve fifty. You leave at twelve fifty-five. Let nobody see you. You go down Great Portland Street. I'll go down Portland Place. Rendezvous at the restaurant at thirteen hundred hours precisely. I've booked a table in the name of Percy Passmore to throw them all off the scent.'

'Should I wear anything distinctive so that you can recognize me?' she says.

'Fancy dress optional,' I say, 'but I should warn you I am wearing no socks today.'

'You'll have to guess what I'm not wearing,' she says.

'Really?' I say, with genuine interest.

'In your dreams, Chris. In your dreams.'

'Thirteen hundred hours,' I repeat. 'Let us synchronize watches.'

* * *

In my befuddled post-lunch state, the sound of my phone ringing confuses me for an instant. There are two ringing tones – one for internal calls and one for external. This one is external, I think. Wine at lunchtime is a bad idea.

'Royal Society for Medical Education,' I say, in my best external manner.

'Now, Christian, what is the Society going to do about George Magwitch?'

I do not need to ask who this is. The clipped delivery, the self-certainty, the stamina to lecture me for the next half-hour – it is Barbara Proudie.

She runs an organisation set up, ostensibly, to fight for victims of medical negligence of all sorts. In practice it seems to exist mainly to provide grief for George Magwitch and a few close friends, of which I (in Barbara's view) have the good fortune to be one.

'When is the Society going to conduct a full inquiry into his research?' she demands. 'This is the medical establishment closing ranks again, Christian. I have evidence that he did not obtain proper consent, but you do nothing about it. People could have died just so that he could test some crackpot theory.'

She runs through his crackpot theory, though I do of course know it quite well. We've had this conversation before, or at least one very much like it. Soon it will be my turn to tell her what she already knows.

'A lot of other researchers were working on the same idea,' I say. 'It wasn't that outlandish. He was simply the first one brave enough to run a clinical trial. And there is no good evidence that consent was not obtained.'

'Do you know what your responsibilities are under your Royal Charter, Christian?' she asks. The answer is: 'No, nor do I give a stuff.' But again, there is no need for me to say anything.

'You have a public duty,' she says, 'to ensure that charlatans like George Magwitch are not allowed to continue to practise. You should carry out a full investigation of all of his research, including the faked data.'

'He was investigated by others and cleared,' I manage to say, when she is obliged to take a breath.

'It was a whitewash.'

'But if we investigate him and clear him, you'll say that's a whitewash too,' I point out.

'If you do it properly, you won't clear him, because he is guilty,' she says triumphantly. 'And do you know what his evidence did to Dan Smith?'

'Roughly,' I say. At the moment, I'm frankly more concerned about what Digby Spain is going to do to me. A lot more concerned.

'They sacked Dan Smith from the care home. He was prosecuted for assault – all because of George Magwitch's trumped-up evidence,' says Barbara.

'But George Magwitch just produced a factual report about the injuries he examined,' I say.

'In a way that made it clear that it could only have been Dan Smith who committed them. Juries listen to expert witnesses, particularly plausible ones with nice accents like George Magwitch. He made up his mind that it was Dan Smith, and ignored everything else that was clearly wrong with that care home.'

I'm not sure that's entirely true – I seem to remember Magwitch laying into the home's management as well. You can accuse George of bias, but nobody's ever accused him of cowardice or half-measures. I get to point out some of this before I am interrupted.

'You should call him to account and then take away his Fellowship of the Society.'

'I'm not sure we can do that, Barbara.'

'By-law 27 (1) b,' she says.

'Oh, right,' I say. Interesting. I'll need to check that one.

'It's not just me. We've got an MP involved in the case now. There will be questions asked in the House.'

'Uhuh,' I say.

And so on and so on, for ever probably if I let her.

I discovered a long time ago that it makes very little difference whether I take part in these conversations or not. If I say nothing, Barbara ploughs ahead regardless. If I say something she ignores it or snorts derisively. She's a really easy person to talk to.

I wonder what it is deep in her past that makes her do this. What triggered a desire to pursue nice doctors in this way? I have met her once. She has iron-grey hair, tied back so tightly that it must hurt. She has a sharp nose that she holds slightly elevated, in order to look down it. And in her eyes there shines the certainty of the righteous. Where have I seen that look before? Ah, yes, it was the last time I saw George Magwitch.

After twenty minutes or so she starts to flag a little and I manage to say: 'I'm sorry, Barbara, I have a meeting to go to.'

'And I,' she says, 'must go and continue to fight for the rights of patients – doing your work for you.'

'Thanks for that,' I say. 'It's really good of you.'

But she too has hung up.

Fatima looks round my door.

'You ought to be at the Parliamentary Affairs Committee,' she says. 'Lucy has already gone.'

I groan and gather my papers together. Then I plod up the stairs towards the graveyard of lost hope that men call Committee Room 2.

8

Neuburg, Danube Valley, November 1619

The waiter knocked on the oak door and carefully pushed it open. In one hand he had a bowl of hot rabbit stew and a hunk of bread. In the other he had a small flask containing some of the straw-coloured local wine and as much of the dubiously coloured local river as the cook thought they could get away with.

'Supper, good sir,' he said jovially. 'The cook has prepared this rich and nutritious mess for you with his own hands. And I have brought it to you with mine. *Service charge at your discretion.* Would you like it over there by the stove? It's a bit warmer out there today, but it's still cold enough to freeze the balls off a wooden donkey, as they say in Oberhausen.'

'Put it anywhere,' said Descartes. 'Just leave it. I'll eat it when I've finished writing this page.'

'That's the proof of God's existence you've got there then?'

'Yes,' said Descartes.

'And therefore of mine?'

'Yes,' said Descartes.

'Better not lose it then,' said the waiter, 'although I have thought further about the problem with your argument.'

Descartes looked up wearily. 'Go on.'

'You say that God, being perfect, must have the property of existence?'

'Quite so.'

'So, doesn't that also leave the way open for a non-existent, imperfect God? Or indeed, since the property of existence is not dependent on perfection, an existent, imperfect God? In which case, aren't you basically stuffed? Because your imperfect God might be deceiving you about the nature of existence, and the rest of reality just goes up in a puff of smoke.'

'Not really—'

'Once you've decided that the only thing you can be certain of is your own existence, then it seems to me that you are stuck on a lonely rock in a sea of uncertainty, with only a few triangles and other abstractions to keep you company.'

'Just put the stew down and piss off,' said Descartes. 'If the roads are any better in the morning, I'm going to see if I can press on to Frankfurt.'

'The river's starting to thaw anyway,' said the waiter, placing the flask of wine on the table.

Back in the warm and steamy kitchen, the waiter reported to the cook that their guest was about to depart.

'Just as well,' said the cook. 'There's an Englishman just arrived looking for a room. We can give him that one.'

'As long as it's not another bloody philosopher,' said the waiter. 'What's his name?'

'Hobbes,' said the cook. 'He says he's called Thomas Hobbes.'

9

Great Portland Street Station, 29 April this Year

I have been skilfully hiding behind my copy of *Metro* since King's Cross, and now allow Jon to descend to the platform before I make a sudden dash and squeeze out between the closing doors. Jon is thus at least a dozen places ahead of me in the crowd that trudges reluctantly up the stairs and towards their respective and much-loathed workplaces. Halfway up, the stairs divide and send us arbitrarily right or left. Tourists sometimes halt at this point, irritated commuters blindly piling up behind them, wondering which way leads to the exit. Both ways do. The crowd is reunited into a single stream as it reaches the top of the stairs and is momentarily checked by the automatic barriers. By some disparity in the speed of flow, my streamlet hits the barriers a few seconds ahead of the other, and I (lurking at the back of my group) find myself face to face with Jon (at the head of his).

'Hi,' I say.

'Good morning, Chris. I didn't see you on the train.'

'No, I didn't see you either.' I wonder if we are both lying. I doubt that he wants to talk to me any more than I want to talk to him. But we've got each other for the five-minute walk to the Society.

'How's the family?' I ask. One day I shall manage to remember the names of his children. Owen, Charity and Helena? Yes, that's it.

'Ben's still sick,' he says. 'I think Faith looks as though she's coming down with the same thing. Ros has had to stay, at home to look after them.' Right, so that's: children = Ben, Faith and A. N. Other. I wonder if I will remember long enough to make a note when I get to work. Probably not.

We approach the pedestrian crossing. If the lights change to green just as we get there then Digby Spain will not stitch me up. They stay red for a long time.

'Database User Group meeting today,' I say, tapping my foot and watching for the red man to change to a green man.

'You don't need *me* for that, do you?' asks Jon. He is not needed and has no intention of coming whatever I say, so what I say is: 'Absolutely. It would be really good if you could get there, Jon.'

'No, better not,' he says, looking along Euston Road for any break in the traffic. 'I need to work on the press release Ethics and Rights Committee want to put out. The draft they've given me is a bit of a mess.'

'Do you know anything about Humph?' I ask.

Jon turns and looks at me, puzzled. 'In what way?'

'He looks really ill.'

'He looks tired.'

'He as good as told me he was dying.'

'Good grief,' says Jon. 'Dying of what?'

I realize I don't know. I shrug in a way that suggests that I am regrettably sworn to secrecy.

Jon seems genuinely upset, and I wonder vaguely why my own reaction a day or so before had merely been surprise. Humph's a good guy, after all.

'Better not say anything to anyone else,' I say.

'No,' says Jon with a frown. 'I won't. But all the same . . .'

'It's not important,' I say.

Jon looks at me oddly. 'Not *important*?'

'I mean, it's confidential,' I say.

'But . . .' he says.

Suddenly a gap appears in the traffic. We sprint across to the central reservation just behind a bus and just ahead of an enormous lorry that is travelling faster than either of us realized. The lorry gives us a long burst of its horn, but it is wasting its time. It can't kill me. That's one thing I'm absolutely certain of. Nothing can kill me. Ever.

'By the way,' says Jon, as if this close brush with death has just reminded him of another unavoidable obligation, 'Ros and I have been meaning to invite you round to dinner. Would the Tuesday after next suit you? You could come back with me, straight from work.'

We are paused on the central reservation, waiting for the second set of lights to change to green.

'That would be good,' I say, realizing that I have already forgotten the names of his children, possibly vital information for a credible visit to his house. Bob and Hope? No, that's not likely. I'll ask Lucy. She'll know. She knows things like that.

The lights on the other side of the central reservation cease for a moment to be red or anything else, and then become green. We stroll across and progress towards the Society in a thoughtful fashion, without further discussion of families (in which I am ill-equipped to take part) or of death (about which I know slightly more than I would wish).

* * *

Names are funny things. I've never met Digby Spain in the flesh, but his moniker conjures up this rather plump upper-class Englishman in a checked waistcoat – an Englishman beginning to go bald and slightly short of breath. His face is round and . . . well . . . more eggshell than gloss, but smooth and probably quite pink. Of course, if I should ever meet him I shall probably find that he is tall, cadaverous and has shoulder-length hair, but I doubt it. Give somebody a name like that and they grow into the part. It's much the same as Virginia, which is, as I have said, quite a name to live up to. A name like that has to be constantly at the back of your mind. I've wanted the Society to carry out scientific research on the subject. You would take identical twins and name one Dominic or Justin, and the other Wayne or LeeRoy and study them as they grew up. The gratuitous cruelty of this experiment might mean that we failed to get Ethics Committee approval, but I think it would be worth a try, just to annoy Barbara Proudie. My last name is interesting in the sense that nobody here knows how to pronounce it or even spell it. It ought to be spelt Sørensen, but since I'd be the only one who would know that was pronounced any differently from Sorensen, I can't be arsed, frankly. My first name, too, was supposed to have three distinct Danish syllables – not two slurred English ones. I think if I had insisted on Christian Sørensen (spelling and pronunciation) I would have a totally different self-image – Nordic, clean-cut, brooding. But as it is . . .

Nicknames are something else again. Like Fat Dave, you end up with what you deserve. Virginia used to call me 'Puppy' at one time, and then stopped. I suppose it meant that I was cute, messy and nipped your trouser leg when you least expected it. I never came up with a pet name for her, and if I'm going to dump her, it isn't really worth the effort now.

* * *

Dumping your girlfriend by email. Yes, absolutely, it's the modern way to do it. More caring than a text message. Less traumatic than a phone call. Cheaper than a final dinner at a flash restaurant and with less danger of miscommunication.

So:

Dear Virginia,

I doubt that this email will come as a surprise to you. You must have noticed how we have been growing apart lately. It's not your fault. You need somebody more mature than I am. You need somebody who is ready to make a lifetime commitment. I on the other hand am not sure what I want or need. I am not Mr Right. I am not even Mr OK. One of the few things Dave has said that you'll agree with (even-

tually) is that you deserve better than me. I am offering
you the chance to find that person. Virginia, you are a
wonderful woman who will one day make some lucky man
a wonderful wife. I hope you can forgive me and that we
can remain friends.
With much affection, Chris

I read it through. Yes, not bad at all. I haven't even
resorted to: 'It's not you, it's me.' Of course I won't send it
today. I press SAVE and then double-check that I haven't sent
it by mistake. No – it's there, safe in my DRAFTS file until I
need it.

* * *

'By *email*?'

'It has certain advantages.'

'Only over a text message, you moron,' says Dave. 'It has
no advantages in any other sense. Would she dump you by
email?'

I consider this carefully. The answer is 'no', obviously.
Virginia would not dump me at all.

'So, you think I should just tell her?' I ask.

'I think you should marry her,' says Dave.

'Marry?' I say. Words like this are not supposed to occur
in our conversations, other than in the context of dire warn-
ings of impending ruin. Then the light begins to dawn. 'Has
Megan brainwashed you? Or . . . oh, my God . . . has your
body been taken over by alien life forms? Dave, we can still
save you. Dave, are you still in there?'

'You're a sad bastard,' says Dave, not unkindly.

'OK, that's agreed then,' I say. 'The email goes off tomorrow at zero nine hundred hours.'

Dave shakes his head. 'What *is* your problem, Chris?' he asks. 'Exactly what *is* your problem?'

10

No Time, No Date

Although I cannot remember exactly when I ceased to believe in reality, I can remember, to the minute, when my childhood ended.

I was in my last year at university. My brother, Niels, was still at school. I had my final exams shortly after Easter and I had decided to stay in Bristol and revise rather than go home. My parents had proposed a week's holiday in the Lake District and, a little to my surprise, had said that if I did not want to join them, they and Niels would go anyway. Having grown up on a small flat island, my parents loved the mountains. I suppose I was surprised only because I found it difficult to imagine them doing anything at all without me. Home was such a fixed and unchanging part of my life that (even though I believed in reality in those days) I could have believed they went into suspended animation as I closed the front door and did not resume their activities until I opened it again at the end of term. It is true that in the meantime a new picture might have been hung or a cup been broken, but these small adjustments only re-emphasized the larger immutability of their lives.

The night before they set off I called them from a phone booth in the hall of residence. My mother explained that they were planning to leave very early to miss the London traffic. My father was outside checking the car and Niels was upstairs finishing packing. They gave me a number on which I could call them in Grasmere – this was in the days before mobile phones made everyone instantly obtainable. I noted the number, but I knew the place already. We had stayed there before.

I woke the following morning before it was light and thought of them, pleased to be up early and missing the traffic, driving north as the sky brightened and became pale blue and pink – newborn colours – excited and looking forward to walking the fells that afternoon. Soon they would be stopping for breakfast, getting out of the car and smelling the fresh cold April air and smiling at each other. I wished that I had gone with them. I have wished the same thing every day since.

If I had gone, then they might have left a few moments earlier or a few moments later. I might have told my father a joke and he might have laughed and driven a bit slower or a bit faster as a result. I might have suggested stopping earlier or later. They would certainly have been somewhere else when the Mini pulled out in front of the lorry and the lorry swerved across two lanes and then skidded sideways along all three. At that moment most places were better than the place they were in.

After breakfast I went to the library. I saw the Warden of

my hall on the way and he commiserated with me for still being there revising and I commiserated with him because he had to write a paper for a conference. I spent the morning on Shakespeare's Sonnets (ABAB CDCD EFEF GG), had lunch at a pub and then went back to the library until it closed. As I left, I realized that my family would have already returned to their guesthouse after that first walk, and would now be changing for dinner. They would have it in the small dining room in which the four of us had eaten so many times before.

It was eleven o'clock in the evening – three minutes past eleven to be precise – when the knock came at my door. As soon as I opened it and saw the Warden, I didn't need to check my watch to know that it was not a social call. His face was grey – actually grey. Even though I guessed in part what he had to say, it was him that I felt sorry for. It was a tough thing that he was going to have to explain.

There had been sixteen cars in the crash that morning. As each piled into the ones in front, the cars that had hit the lorry first were pounded again and again into strange and wonderful shapes, unlike anything their owners could have possibly imagined when they purchased them. The rescue services had thought at first that it was fifteen, but eventually, as they pulled the lorry upright, they found my parents' car, crushed almost beyond recognition as a piece of machinery. After a while they also worked out that there had been three people in the car. There should by rights have been four, but as it happened there were just the three. That's why it took a while to track me down: a whole day when my parents and my brother were still alive for me, walking the fells, telling each other silly jokes, eating dinner in that small over-heated dining room in the guesthouse with the picture of Kendal Fair over the mantelpiece, complimenting the land-lady on how cosy (*hyggelig*) it all was. A whole extra day's life, in fact.

The university asked me if I wanted to delay taking my exams, but I just said: What's the point? I got a First, but when I collected the degree later that year, there was nobody of any importance to see me receive it.

That was the day my childhood ended, and that was the day that I knew that I was not intended to die – because dying would have been so easy, but I wasn't allowed to. That was also the day when I realized that families could not be trusted. However much you loved them, they could desert you suddenly and without warning, leaving nothing in their place. Later I realized that for 'families' you could just insert the word 'people'. Have as little to do with them as possible. That's my advice.

the length of her skirt, without any regard to her committee or other experience?

Yes, of course I was.

* * *

It's six thirty and time to go home if I am not to be late for Lucy. I open the DRAFTS box and see that my provisional girlfriend-dumping email is still there. But I won't send it. I'll delete it now. The next time Virginia phones I shall tell her and nothing she says will make any difference. I shall make a clean break.

The phone rings. I pick it up (as you do).

'It's my father,' says Virginia. 'He's had a heart attack. I need you to drive me to Horsham.'

'But . . .' I begin. Can I respond by saying: 'Certainly, and you're dumped, by the way'? Possibly not.

'I'll explain when I see you,' she says.

In the background I can hear somebody talking and then Virginia saying something that sounds like: 'No, it's better this way. Really, Harry.' Then she's speaking to me again. 'Chris? Are you still there?'

'Yes, I'm obviously still here. Three seconds isn't long enough to go anywhere else. But where are you?' I say.

'A bar. I've been having a few drinks with friends. Quite a few. That's why I can't drive myself. Mum just rang me on my mobile. Chris, can you do it?'

'OK, where is this bar?'

'Clerkenwell, but it doesn't matter. I'll see you at my flat as soon as you can get there. We'll take my car.'

110

11

Great Portland Street Station, May Day Morn

It's Friday and, as if to offer some symmetry to the past fortnight, Narinder taps me on the shoulder as I am leaving the station.

'First day of the month.' He beams.

'Yes,' I say. 'Don't your people dance round the maypole or something this morning?'

'My people?'

'The English,' I say.

'Not round Hackney,' he says.

Appearances can be deceptive. Take me and Narinder. If you saw us together you'd say he was the immigrant and that my family had been around since King Ethelred's time. Actually, he's third-generation British, his grandfather having come over to study medicine and never quite got round to going back to India. I, on the other hand, wasn't even born here. English is my second language, even if I have largely

107

forgotten my first. I'm a genuine ethnic minority, albeit a very small one.

We walk along for a bit. Narinder is dressed in his usual office gear: a V-necked sweater, white shirt, grey trousers, cheap tie. It could be the uniform of a very downmarket school. He carries a briefcase, which I suspect has nothing in it except his sandwiches. I am dressed smartly but casually in a black T-shirt, with some wooden beads that I picked up in Goa last year. Black Levi's. Hemp shoulder bag. No brief-case. Absolutely no socks.

'Chris, can I take six weeks' leave this summer?' Narinder asks suddenly.

'Have you got six weeks?'

'I carried some over, remember?'

'Amritsar?'

He looks embarrassed. 'Yeah.'

'They'll marry you off to some nice Sikh girl while you're there.'

This is the risk that we both know about. Nothing to do with the unavailability of hamburgers. He looks even more embarrassed and says: 'Yeah.'

'Fine,' I say. 'Let me have your leave card to sign.'

'Do you ever think about getting married, Chris?'

'I think about it all the time,' I say. 'But not in a good way.'

* * *

Today we have Ethics and Rights. Yesterday,
We had Media Board. And tomorrow morning,
We shall have Publications Sub-committee. But today,

Today we have Ethics and Rights. The sunshine
Gleams off ivy on the Regent's Park railings
And today we have Ethics and Rights.

This is the UN Convention and this
Is the Society response to the Government statement
Which you will see the point of when the Governmen
    issue it,
Which they haven't yet. The branches
Of the lilac trees issue beyond the railings
Hinting we are missing the point.
Here is the list of meetings of this committee,
For the rest of the year. And please do not tell me
You are already tied up. You were notified by email
Weeks ago. Spring is here but the rest of my life,
Is tied up in lists of committees and sub-committee
For today we have Ethics and Rights.

I wonder if 'ivy' is the right word. It sort of scans ally I can't see any from where I am sitting, though floor there is a good view. I can see holly, but tha wrong connotations – Christmas and so on, thou ously there is holly all the year round, a bit like rol up' isn't quite right either. 'Engaged'? Hmm.

'Did you get that last action point, Chris?' asks man of the Ethics and Rights Committee.

'Absolutely,' I say, looking up and nodding to the whole bearded gathering. Actually, Lucy supposed to be minuting this, so I'll find out fro wards what that was all about. Of course, th chance that Lucy's mind will have been elsewhe wise, I wonder, to appoint an assistant purely o

I am already closing files, saving things, switching off my computer.

'I'm coming right over,' I say.

* * *

The roads are strangely empty under the yellow glare of the street lights, as if nothing dares impede our progress. Virginia stares straight ahead, willing her father to stay alive until she reaches Horsham. She didn't say much at the flat and is saying even less now, but it does not sound good. Her mother is with her father at the hospital. Nobody is expecting he'll last the night. But what do they know? What does anyone know? At least she's not crying. Please, please, don't let her cry yet.

People pass by on the pavements of South London. They look real enough. Only René Descartes and I know they are not. A well-thought-out Indian family is standing outside Nancy Lam's restaurant, mother, father, three children, smartly dressed, all talking to each other at once. How odd that they have been constructed just so that I can drive past them now; then, in a flash, their brief moment of existence will be over. I watch them receding in my rear-view mirror and they disappear for ever. Gone. They've had their ten seconds of fame.

'What are you thinking about?' asks Virginia suddenly.

It's going to be a difficult one to answer, so I say: 'I was just thinking how unreal this all is.'

'I know,' she says. 'It was just so unexpected. I can't quite believe what's happened. In a strange way it's reassuring you feel like that too.'

That wasn't what I meant, but it's not easy to explain what I did mean, so I let it go.

'Your father has always been very good to me,' I say. 'Like a father . . .'

My voice tails off, leaving this strange oxymoron hanging in mid-air.

'I never met your father,' says Virginia.

Obviously, I know this. 'No,' I say.

'You've never told me much about the accident your parents died in.'

'No,' I say.

Her hand stretches out and touches my arm briefly, in a gesture that says that she sympathizes, respects my privacy and hopes my pain will go away. Only girls can pack all of that into a single gesture, in my experience. Of course, it is a gesture only in respect of my parents. She doesn't know about Niels. I've never told her about Niels. I am not going to start thinking about Niels now.

I rub my hand across my eyes and accelerate away from Dorking, curving off the big roundabout and onto the dual carriageway. For Virginia's sake I want to get to the hospital while Hugh is still alive; on the other hand, I suddenly realize, I don't particularly want to be there to watch him die. I've done the whole death thing in triplicate, and it's no fun at all. Honestly. Suddenly I am terrified that I shall have to sit there and watch him die. I feel my foot ease off on the accelerator again.

'Sixty speed limit,' says Virginia, automatically, staring once again into the night and the unfathomable future.

No, it's time for me to do the grown-up thing. I push the

accelerator to the floor and make police siren noises. 'Stuff the speed limit,' I say. 'This is the express service to Horsham.'

* * *

In the end, Hugh died as considerately as he lived. I dropped Virginia at the hospital entrance and she was there with him at the end. By the time I had found somewhere to park the car, it was all over. He'd granted both of us our wishes. He was good like that.

A strange thought occurred to me as we left the hospital: if Hugh did have another Woman, then he'd taken that particular secret to the grave. Of course, at this precise point in the story, I'd still no idea that there were plenty of other secrets where that one came from. That was being saved up for later.

It was almost midnight as I drove Virginia and her mother the few miles back to their house. It seemed wrong to be driving away from the hospital leaving Hugh there, but all logic pointed to a good night's sleep before we started to focus on the telephoning, form filling and miscellaneous bureaucracy that is such an important part of dying in the twenty-first century.

* * *

A good night's sleep is not, however, immediately on offer.

'I think we all need a drink,' says Virginia, as she closes the front door with its little stained-glass window and locks it (how many times did Hugh do that?) 'I could do with one anyway.'

She goes to Hugh's drinks cupboard, takes out a heavy cut-glass tumbler and pours a large measure of brandy into it. She looks at the two of us. I shrug. Maybe Daphne just wants to go to bed.

'I'll have a Bailey's,' says Daphne, with a sudden and fierce determination. 'A very large one.'

'I'll do it,' I say. I pour her quite a lot of the creamy brown liquid, but she just passes the glass back to me and says: 'No, a *large* one.' I figure it will help her sleep, so I empty the bottle. I fetch Hugh's malt whisky from the back of the cupboard. I can almost hear Hugh's voice saying: 'Drink it, Chris. For God's sake, drink it. Daphne will only use it for cooking or something.' OK. Let's all get drunk then.

I've never seen Daphne drink alcohol before and I suspect that, like others who are unused to it, she will badly misjudge its effect. I keep my eye on the fine lead crystal in her hand, ready to catch it when she drops off to sleep and it starts to slip from her fingers. You don't want to spill Bailey's on the Axminster or spend the following day trying to locate the last of the needle-like shards of broken glass. She shows no sign of falling asleep however. Quite the reverse. Though she is talking to me about mundane things, a steely glint is appearing in her eye, a determination to do something. But what? Virginia too seems to be silently building up to making some announcement. It's just a question of which of them gets to it first.

Virginia's opening line is low key. 'It's funny not having

Dad here,' she says. 'But I can almost feel him looking down on us. I sort of wonder where he is now.'

I take this to mean, Do good souls go straight to heaven or do they hang around for a bit, checking out who's making off with their gold watch or stamp collection? It's the strange sort of thought that is comfortingly appropriate for this hour of the morning. Daphne's reply, however, alerts me to the fact that we may be heading for wacky, uncharted territory.

'Yes, I've often wondered where your father was,' she says. She gives a long sigh and then a sort of hiccup.

Daphne looks at both of us with the apologetic smile of somebody who does not yet realize they have had too much to drink but is going to very soon. I turn to look at Virginia and notice that she is already looking at me, so we both turn to look at Daphne, who isn't looking at either of us any more.

'Well,' says Daphne, when we have finished looking. 'I suppose we could all do with some sleep.' She puts down her glass, trying to conceal the fact that it is still half full of Bailey's. She attempts to stand up but has forgotten how she used to do it.

'What do you mean?' asks Virginia very slowly. 'You've often wondered where my father was?'

'Just sometimes,' says Daphne. 'Not all the time.' She clearly feels this explanation is sufficient, because she tries to stand up again. This time she almost makes it.

People sometimes say that I am unperceptive, but it has already occurred to me that this is a conversation I should stay well out of.

'What do you mean?' asks Virginia again. Something tells

me that she is going to get to the bottom of this. 'Dad's hardly been out of your sight since you married him, except to go to work.'

Daphne is frowning, trying to figure out how to explain it. 'You see,' she says, after a long pause, 'the thing is this: your dad's not your father.'

In one sense it's a bit like saying two plus two does not equal four, but in all other respects, it cuts straight to the chase.

As you will have noticed, it is the sort of statement that requires clarification only if you can't or don't want to believe what you've just heard. 'Dad's *not* my father?' asks Virginia, seeking clarification.

'Hugh is not your real dad,' says Daphne. I wonder if she could have said that sober, but she looks relieved to have said it at all.

'Then . . .' says Virginia.

'Who is?' Daphne nods to herself. 'Malcolm Biggenhalgh. What a bastard. What a *total* bastard. But I loved him, so there it is.' Daphne turns to me as if I might be able to back up her story. I nod reassuringly to confirm Malcolm Biggenhalgh is the biggest bastard in the Home Counties. It's the polite thing to do. Strangely, I'm pretty certain that I *do* know somebody called something like that, though, if I'm right, it's unlikely to be the same guy. There is now a tear (for somebody) forming at the corner of one eye, which Daphne makes no attempt to wipe away. She successfully locates her glass and consumes her recommended intake of alcohol for the next seven days in a single swallow. She looks thoughtful, then gives a small burp, and for the first time this evening appears slightly embarrassed at her conduct.

'So, where is he now?' I say.

Daphne looks at me as though I have just asked a very interesting question. 'Do you know,' she says, 'I've *often* wondered that.'

* * *

I am in bed with Virginia. For the first time we are lying side by side under the white crocheted bedspread in Hugh and Daphne's (now just Daphne's) guest bedroom, though neither of us is doing anything special to celebrate the fact. Virginia is already asleep, snoring softly (though she claims that I alone snore). Daphne too is in bed and almost certainly in a Bailey's-induced slumber, dreaming of . . . whom? Only I am alert, with the events of the day going through my mind.

I am sleeping with the girl that I am supposed to have dumped. In the meantime, I remember with a stab of guilt, Lucy will have been waiting for me at my flat for about six hours – unless she has given up by now and gone home, which is (on reflection) probable, though she looks like the sort of girl who might hang around for six hours to make her point. It is thus quite possible that on Monday I shall experience girl-rage from a new source, girl-rage that may not be measurable under the Sorensen-Birtwistle Revised Classification and for which an entirely new scale may have to be constructed. She'll cut off my head (or some other convenient part of my anatomy) and staple it to Passmore's Staff

Suggestions Box. Also, she probably won't tell me the names of Jon's children.

On the plus side, of course, if Lucy kills me then I shall not have to take responsibility for the Digby Spain fiasco nor shall I have to experience Jon's silent smugness on any of the above. On the minus side, I shall be dead. I weigh the options up without coming to any definite conclusions.

So, I lie awake a little longer wondering if there is some third way that I have not thought of. I could, of course, just not show up at the office on Monday, but I'd need a good excuse.

Little do I know it, but just such an excuse is winging its way towards me through the mild Sussex night.

12

Horsham, Saturday

I awake to the sound of birdsong and the trees gently rustling outside the window. The sun is shining through a gap in the curtains. There is a warm and apparently naked body beside mine under the white bedspread. I am not quite sure where I am, but it seems that I am being rewarded for being good in this or (more likely) a previous life. Then one by one the lead balls fall into place with a clunk.

1. I am in Horsham.
2. I am here because Hugh is dead.
3. I have not dumped Virginia.
4. Lucy is going to kill me in the near future.
5. If she doesn't, Humph will.

I am hoping that there are no more lead balls left, then I remember:

6. Hugh is not, and never has been, Virginia's father.

I don't yet fully understand in what way the last of these is my problem, but I expect that I shall understand very shortly. Also I really think I did once know somebody called Malcolm Biggenhalgh, but that is one complication too many. I go back to the top of the list and work my way down again. The only good thing is that, however bad number six may prove to be, it is not as bad as numbers two to five.

It's already half past eight. I get up and dress sufficiently not to alarm Daphne, then I go down to the kitchen and make tea for her. I imagine that Hugh has been contractually obliged to do this since he got married and, somehow, having tea brought to her this morning may make things a little easier. Or not. But I need activity or I may start screaming, which would not be good in a house of sorrow and mourning.

In the kitchen I make tea and send Lucy a text message that reads: **'Sorry last night. Unexpected problem, Horsham. Will phone soonest. C.'** I decide the safe thing would be not to phone until I see Lucy's response. I wonder whether I was wise to admit to being in Horsham, but I figure it's quite a large town and there will be plenty of policemen around on a Saturday morning.

I knock cautiously on Daphne's door. If she's still asleep, then it's probably because she needs as much sleep as she can get, and I plan just to leave the tea and silently tiptoe away. But she's sitting up in bed as though she was expecting this all along. She shows no signs of having the hangover that she richly deserves. So I end up sitting on the edge of the bed, on a rose-embroidered bedspread that must be forty years old, while she sips her tea.

'I probably said a few things that I shouldn't have last night,' she says. She's good at understatements, is Daphne.

'I don't know,' I say. 'It's not for me to judge.'

'You see,' she continues, 'Hugh liked you a lot. He'd always hoped that you and Virginia would get married, though I understand how things are now.'

I wonder for a moment if she can read my mind and she knows that I am planning to dump her daughter. If so, she seems quite laid back about it really – cool. Or maybe she just means that people tend to live with each other rather than get married these days. Or maybe . . .

'What do you mean: how things are?' I say, not really wanting an answer.

'Well . . .' she says, not really giving me one. 'That's what we'd *both* hoped really. Hugh saw you as the son he never had, just as Virginia was the daughter he never had.' She gives a little sigh and goes on: 'I had to tell her. I couldn't let her go all the way through the funeral thinking that Hugh was her father. You should only have to bury a father once.'

I nod. Not burying your father more than once seems a good plan.

'Because Malcolm *is* her father. When she was younger, we couldn't say anything, of course, but I made up my mind: if anything happened to either of us, the first thing I would have to do was tell Virginia about Malcolm. Then again, Malcolm might have died years ago and none of us will be able to go to his funeral anyway, which would be a pity.' She gives a much longer sigh than before and takes a thoughtful sip of tea. I am beginning to realize that this is not just about

Virginia and her real father. A great deal of it is about Daphne and Malcolm.

'He was a bit younger than me,' she says. 'You don't call people "dashing" any more, do you? But that's what he was. Dashing. He had an MG. I don't think he knew I was pregnant when he dumped me, but I'm not sure it would have made much difference if he had. Then suddenly there was Hugh, telling me that he'd always loved me . . . There was only one thing I could do really. Being a single mother on benefits wasn't the glamorous thing then that it is today. I never told Malcolm that Virginia was his, but he must have worked it all out. Even men can count. He came to the wedding, obviously.'

'Obviously,' I say.

'He went his way and we went to Horsham,' Daphne continues. 'It seemed like a good place to bring up Virginia. There were schools.'

'Farlington,' I say.

'She got a scholarship. She was school captain. Three grade As. She loved Farlington. She was really happy there.'

There is a long pause. She looks towards the window. The birdsong in the garden outside is almost deafening.

'So, I've often wondered where he was,' says Daphne.

I go back down to the kitchen and this time make coffee for Virginia. She too is awake and ready to take delivery of a reviving hot drink.

'Are you OK?' I ask solicitously.

'Where have you been?' she demands in return.

'Talking to your mother.'

'And?'

'Malcolm dumped her, but she still loves him.'

'She told you that?'

'She didn't have to,' I say. I tell her what I know.

'Did she say where Malcolm was?'

'He went his way.'

'Could be anywhere then, other than here.'

'Pretty much,' I say.

'I have to find him,' she says. She's been thinking about it. Thinking is not always a good idea. 'He's been out there all that time and I've known nothing about him.'

There we are: another plot ticking away in the background, waiting to spring itself on me. You think you've got all of the parents you need, then another one jumps up out of nowhere.

'He sort of deserted you,' I say.

'He deserted my mother,' she says. So that's all right then.

'We can hardly go looking for him now,' I say. 'We've got a funeral to arrange.'

'True,' she says.

The conversation is fairly slow over the cornflakes. Virginia says: 'Pass the milk,' and Daphne passes the sugar. Virginia says: 'No, the *milk*,' and Daphne, apologizing, picks up the milk and pours some into her own coffee. Then she pauses and says: 'Sorry, was it toast that you wanted?' You might say that we're all a bit preoccupied with our own thoughts.

It's Daphne who finally says something almost rational.

'We need to find him – your father, I mean. He ought to be at your dad's funeral.'

'I was thinking the same thing,' says Virginia.

'They were always such good friends – until one of them got me pregnant and the other one had to marry me. Your father, that is.'

'Yes,' says Virginia. At least they understand each other, but I am having difficulty keeping up and, frankly, if you have unwittingly dipped into the story at this point, I'd suggest you backtrack a bit to preserve your sanity.

'They worked together for years. Then your dad sacked your father,' Daphne continues, 'and that was that.'

No, sorry, lost it completely. 'Who sacked who?' I say.

'Dad,' says Virginia.

'. . . sacked her father,' says Daphne.

'You couldn't just call them Hugh and Malcolm, I suppose?'

They both look at me and I say: 'Sorry.'

'*Hugh* sacked *Malcolm*,' says Daphne, as if she were having to explain the two times table. 'It had nothing to do with me. Or maybe it did, who knows? Hugh just came home one day and said he had had to let him go. Wives didn't get to question things like that in those days. We just got on with it.'

I can't see Daphne as Patient Griselda myself – never a convincing story at the best of times and doubly so if set in Horsham – so I just nod.

'I always hoped that they would be reconciled,' says Daphne. 'It would have been nice if they could have gone to each other's funerals.' This is technically impossible, but a good thought.

'He left no forwarding address?' I ask.

'He went north,' says Daphne.

We're in Sussex, I think. From here everywhere is north. But I nod again.

'We can find him,' I say suddenly. Why am I saying this? Can we? Do we want to? I look from one to the other. 'We'll find him in time for the funeral.'

Daphne smiles. Virginia touches my arm, tacitly offering me as much sex as I can handle for ever. 'Thank you,' she says with feeling.

But we don't set out on a madcap road trip that morning. We make lists of people who need to be told and Virginia does a lot of phoning of distant cousins. I obtain from the Internet printouts of 'things to do when a loved one dies'. Grieving is, it seems, not one of them. There is the hospital to visit and a death certificate to obtain. We drop in on an undertaker's – Daphne had spotted it some time ago and noted it 'just in case'. Everyone is very kind. They are especially kind to me because, while Virginia and Daphne are being extremely brave, I am not. When Virginia asks me why I keep sniffing I say that I must be getting hay fever. She says: 'In April?' and I say: 'Why not?' Daphne sees a really pretty black hat and buys it. 'I'm getting to an age when I go to lots of funerals,' she says. 'I'll get good wear out of it.'

We break at lunchtime for three salads. We shall return to the fray on Monday. But the vicar can still be visited in the afternoon. He offers sympathy in a large, untidy office and agrees to officiate. We in return are ungratefully vague about whether he will see us in church on Sunday. He nods, like one who has suffered much disappointment in his life.

We come home tired. I reflect on the fact that death is now arranged in such a way that intense activity can act as an antidote for grief. Daphne says in an inconsequential way that she needs to take a nap. I am about to say something equally inconsequential in return, when I notice that there is a tear running down her cheek. I wonder whether this is the point at which I go up to her and hug her and say that it's OK to feel grief and it's OK not to feel grief and consistency is not, in this respect, a virtue of any sort.

But I don't. I watch her leave the room, the hatbox suspended from one finger by its pale green ribbon. Then I make more coffee. It's the sort of thing I'm good at.

'I'm not trying to duck out of it,' I say, handing Virginia her mug. I am aware of the deal that we have done and the vast amount of implied sexual activity tied up in it, 'but why is it so vital to find Malcolm before the funeral?'

'Mum wants us to. She had a word with me when you were filling in forms at the council offices. She'd really like him there.'

'I still don't see why.'

'I'm not sure I do entirely either. I can understand why she might want to see Malcolm again, but I can't understand why it's important that he is at Hugh's funeral. On the other hand, if it's possible . . .'

'So, you want me to do this for Daphne?'

'No, I want you to do this for Hugh. They seem to have been best friends once upon a time. I don't know why he sacked Malcolm, but Mum says he always felt bad about it. Malcolm at the funeral is a way of drawing a line under it. Maybe in the end, that's why Mum wants him there.'

'I'll do it for Hugh,' I say.

* * *

Just before we go to bed I get a text from Lucy, in reply to mine sent that morning. It is quite short.

It reads: **'Chris, exactly what is your problem?'**

She's got a point.

13

Sunday

When Mr Bennet wishes to track down Lydia and the dastardly George Wickham, he has to set off in a post-chaise (or whatever) for London and tramp the streets. Not so the modern searcher for lost persons. The search for Malcolm Biggenhalgh begins comfortably seated at a desk in Hugh's study. You might have assumed that the twenty-first century would not have had much impact on Hugh and Daphne, but Hugh was quick to spot the advantages of the Internet to the freelance military historian and was wired up even before I was. We therefore have a powerful laptop at our command and a whole world out there.

I try Google first, searching for 'Malcolm Biggenhalgh' and 'M Biggenhalgh'. It is the latter that turns up the wackiest coincidence. There is an M. Biggenhalgh right here in Horsham. We check him out with trepidation – this is scarily easy. He is treasurer of a local parent-teacher association and features two or three times on the school website. On further investigation he (or somebody with the same name) is also a member of a local football team and, according to a newspaper report, was last season's leading goal scorer.

'How old would Malcolm be?' I ask Virginia.

'A couple of years younger than Mum,' she says. 'So, I suppose that means mid-fifties.'

'Not likely, therefore,' I say, reading from the page in front to me, 'to sprint the full length of the pitch and unleash a power-driver of a shot past the flailing arms of the West Chiltington goalkeeper?'

'Did he immediately have a heart attack?'

'It doesn't say. He's also got some very young children, apparently.'

'Probably not then,' she says. 'Who else do you have?'

There are three actual, genuine Malcolm Biggenhalghs featuring on various websites. One died in 1887 and one in 1936, so that rules them out. The third won second prize in a Lake District dog show (or rather his terrier, Scruff, did) but there is tantalizingly little to go on for our only living Malcolm Biggenhalgh.

'We can't go hunting aimlessly round the whole of Cumbria,' says Virginia sensibly, rejecting what was going to be my first suggestion. She stares intently at the screen and tucks a stray wisp of dark hair behind her ear. Why have I never noticed before that she is beautiful? Has she changed over the past twenty-four hours or have I? For an instant I stare at her staring at Hugh's laptop, then I return to the job in hand, because that's what we're doing.

'All we know is that he was there for a dog show,' I say. 'People travel miles for them. Still, all is not lost.'

I check the electoral rolls online, which you can do at a

small price. We come up with a Malcolm Biggenhalgh in Grasmere. We have an address and we know that another quick search will give us his telephone number. And it's only nine forty-five. We could ring Malcolm, tell him he has a beautiful grown-up daughter and still have time to surprise the vicar by showing up for communion. I suggest this to Virginia.

'But . . .' she says.

'Yes . . .' I reply.

I do immediately see her point. Making contact with your parents for the first time is a special occasion and best done shortly after birth. This call is going to be just a bit of a shock for Malcolm (and Scruff). Serve him right, some might say, but all the same . . .

'He might turn out to be terrible,' she says. 'He could be an alcoholic or a druggie or anything. He could show up stoned and disrupt the funeral. People change . . .'

'So what do you want to do?' I ask. 'Write?'

'I need to think about it,' she says.

'Fine,' I say.

'Can we drive to Grasmere tomorrow?' she says.

'I thought you needed time to think?'

'I've thought,' she says. 'I have to see what he's like, and then decide whether we tell him.'

'How do we do that?' I ask.

'Don't worry, darling. You'll come up with something,' she says.

And she gives me a kiss on my cheek, which is nice.

* * *

Monday opens with a further visit to the funeral parlour and another round of form filling in various offices around town.

Back at the house I send an email to Humph to say that I need leave at short notice to sort out a few things. I wonder whether to email Lucy, but we seem to have said it all by text anyway. If she wants to give me further feedback on my status as a human being, I am sure she will do so in her own good time. So, I email Jon and tell him he's in charge and to let Narinder, Fatima and Lucy know I probably won't be in this week. Virginia phones her office on her mobile, then disappears into the bedroom and talks to somebody for some time.

By late morning we are in a position to hand over control of any forthcoming funerals to Daphne for a couple of days so that we can set off on what is beginning to strike me as a rather strange mission.

But the sun is shining and the blossom on the trees dances as we swish past on our way to London. In a strange way it is good to be here rather than at work. This is what I should be doing: running away from my problems as fast as I possibly can, with no clear plan as to what I shall do when I stop running.

We pause in my flight while Virginia collects a few things from her flat. Then we go on to my flat, above a gym in Essex Road, and collect a few of mine. I also (while Virginia is in the kitchen making coffee) pull out an old file misleadingly marked 'Shakespeare's Sonnets' and verify the contents. I now know why the name Biggenhalgh was vaguely familiar – of course, how could I forget? – but I also know that the man in the file cannot possibly be the one we are going to meet.

'Don't you have *any* clean mugs?' calls a voice from the kitchen.

I push the file quietly back into the obscure place from which it has come and shout: 'They've only had coffee in them.'

In reply, I hear the kitchen tap splashing furiously into the sink. I double-check that the file is invisible to the casual snooper and then wander slowly towards the kitchen and the smell of newly made coffee in spotless mugs.

* * *

We leave Virginia's car in my parking space and take the MG. This trip has to be done properly and that means a classic sports car with a leather gearstick, leaking roof, one good wing mirror and no heating.

We stop for a late lunch at the first service station on the M1 – a quick sandwich amongst the holidaymakers, the lorry drivers, the bikers and the businessmen driving north. Now we are on our way it seems important to be there as soon as possible At Birmingham we join the M6 and I start nervously counting the junctions. I am starting to feel sick. This is worse than I was expecting.

'Could you take over at the next service station?' I ask suddenly.

'You know I can't stand driving this stupid thing,' she says. 'If you wanted me to drive, why didn't we take my car?'

I explain the importance of having a leather gearstick, but she doesn't seem impressed.

'Just for a few miles,' I say.

We swap at the service station. She is not happy. She abruptly turns down my suggestion of coffee as some sort of justification for the stop. She even says that she does not need the loo, which (since she's a girl) cannot possibly be true. I sheepishly relinquish the driver's seat and she sweeps round and takes my place.

'I haven't even got the right shoes on,' she mutters. A Number Fourteen is descending on us – a brooding and well-justified background resentment with flashes of unrelated irritation.

'Sorry,' I mutter, hunching myself up in the passenger seat.

'What have you got your eyes closed for?' she demands as we rejoin the traffic. 'If you don't like the way I drive, then I have to point out that I did not ask to have to steer this rust heap along one of the busiest motorways in the country.'

I open my eyes. 'Your driving is fine. It's just . . .'

'Just what?'

I realize that a short explanation at this point would clear everything up and avoid what seems likely to become a major source of resentment for months to come.

'It's just . . .' I say again. Then I lapse into silence. When I am sure she's not looking, I close my eyes tightly. I wonder if I can hunch myself into a ball and moan gently to myself without Virginia noticing I am doing anything out of the ordinary. Though she is used to my doing odd things, this might be just a shade too much off the wall. Still, in the deepest recesses of my mind where no girlfriend can ever go, I picture myself hunched into a ball and screaming at the top of my voice, as I would rather like to do right now.

14

Heading North

I have had my eyes screwed shut for ten minutes now. Virginia must be deliberately looking elsewhere because she has fired no sarcasm in my direction since just after we left the service station. This is unusual. At some point, obviously, I shall have to open my eyes because:

1. It's getting uncomfortable.
2. I'll look stupid getting out of the car with my eyes closed.

But is it safe yet?

I half-open them, but that's enough to discover exactly where I am. I think: Oh, shit, no.

'What?' asks Virginia.

OK. So I didn't just think it. Try to focus, Christian (three syllables). In spite of appearances, there may be an easy way out of this. I wonder whether I can say that I've just realized I've left my toothbrush behind, or something equally trivial, but I know that if I am going to tell her anything then it has to be the truth. Even if she could be persuaded I care that much about my toothbrush, I am on holy ground (or at least, we've just flashed past holy ground doing seventy-five in the fast lane) and I therefore cannot tell a lie.

I take a deep breath, but my voice is still not really under my own control. 'It was just back there that it happened,' I say. I pause for a second and then jab my finger towards a fast-disappearing junction. 'Exactly there.'

Virginia, driving and perhaps not focusing too much on my finger, looks to her left at an innocent stretch of hard shoulder, bounded by a steep green bank. For her, I have as yet explained nothing.

'What?' she says.

'The red mini came on to the motorway back there,' I say. 'Almost immediately it pulled out to overtake an old Land Rover towing a trailer. The driver didn't see the lorry coming up behind it. The lorry braked and everything else piled into it, including my parents' car. That's where they died.' I realize that I've had this speech prepared for years; the phrase: 'an old Land Rover towing a trailer' is comfortingly rounded and familiar. So is: 'the lorry braked and everything else piled into it'. But I've never actually spoken these precise words to anyone. 'Yes,' I've said to people, in the version I tell, 'that's right. My parents died in an accident. No, it was a long time ago.' So that's OK then: no details needed. My audience tries not to actually sigh with relief. No need to worry about good old Chris. At this point somebody usually offers to buy me a beer.

'You said they died in a car accident,' Virginia begins, 'but you didn't say where . . .'

'Well, the accident had to be *somewhere*,' I say, 'and it

happens to have been *here*. Is that OK with you? *Is* it? Because if it's not . . .' My voice tails off in its turn. In the ensuing silence I punch the dashboard hard with my fist. The fact that Virginia does not comment on the stupidity of this last act speaks volumes for how stupid it actually was. I realize that I've just done the first two stages of grief in the Kübler-Ross model (Denial, Anger) in approximately a minute and a half. I try to remember what the third is. If it's an embarrassing display of emotion, then I'm about to hit the nail right on the head again, because a sort of cough rises up from somewhere deep inside me and I'm sobbing and I can't work out how to stop.

Virginia carefully brings the car to a standstill on the hard shoulder, and now she is hugging me and I'm crying, and she's still hugging me and so on and so on. 'Poor Puppy,' she says, stroking my hair. 'You poor Puppy. But it was a long time ago.' I want to tell her that that is exactly why I'm crying, but I can't stop crying long enough to tell her.

Still, all good things come to an end. Eventually the cough seems to go in reverse, back down inside me, and I am left feeling exhausted and in a strange way cleansed, as if I have just been pummelled and scrubbed within a inch of my life in a Turkish bath in Marrakesh (as indeed I once was – remind me and I'll tell you about it some time). My right hand aches where I hit the dashboard, an act that is beginning to strike even me as inadvisable.

'We'd better get off the hard shoulder and get moving,' says Virginia, 'or there . . .' She doesn't finish the sentence, the last part of which is clearly: '. . . could be a nasty accident.' I appreciate her tact in this matter.

She skilfully rejoins the traffic, in spite of unsuitable footwear and a wonky wing mirror. Everything is drifting calmly up the motorway in the late-afternoon sun – the holidaymakers, the bikers, the lorry drivers, the businessman – all travelling north, all blissfully unaware that they have just passed the site of one of the worst smashes ever on the M6. They pass us, or we pass them, silently, as though we are very far away from each other. My ears seem to have disconnected from my brain. As far as I can tell, I am also saying nothing. Virginia looks across at me, concerned, but maintains a respectful silence.

The sun is already beginning to set when she finally says: 'God, it's been a tough day for you.'

'It could have been worse,' I say, 'but thank you for addressing me as God.'

She turns and laughs. 'Welcome back, Chris,' she says. 'I thought we'd lost you there for a moment.'

* * *

We drive on, with the darkening outline of the Lakeland hills now forming a broad purple band to our left.

Virginia is looking straight ahead. I can read nothing in her expression. I watch the hills fading slowly into a sooty sky and wonder a bit about this grief thing. Virginia and Daphne seem to be handling theirs pretty well, all things considered. On the other hand, so have I for a number of years. Did Daphne really love Hugh, or did she just resent spending the best thirty years of her life with somebody whose favourite book was Swinson's *Register of the Regiments and Corps of the British Army*? Does she still love

Malcolm? Does she know the answers herself? Grief, love . . . what do any of us know?

'I'm glad you told me about your parents at last,' says Virginia. 'I know how hard it was for you, but it helps to talk about these things.'

I nod. It helps to talk about these things. But I still haven't told her about Niels. I know that I shall never be able to tell her about Niels.

* * *

We have passed though Ambleside and are now following a road running along the shore of Rydal Water. I am driving again on the grounds that I am no longer, for the time being anyway, a gibbering wreck of a human being. Virginia is trying to read the map book in the rapidly fading light.

'It looks as if we're almost there,' she says. 'We should be able to find somewhere to stay in Grasmere. Then let's get a bite to eat, my little Puppy, and plan for tomorrow.'

'I've already got plans for where we're going to stay,' I tell her.

You have to know how to spot it – you come round the bend with the high rocks and overhanging trees masking everything, and suddenly the lake is there to your left and the guesthouse is on the right. I just have time to note the sign saying: '*Vacancies*'. I indicate, slow and pull onto the gravel in front of the house. 'Here?' asks Virginia, looking up at the grey, rectangular, solidly built structure in front of us. It looks a sound choice but, apart from its location right on the water, it is to all appearances no better and no worse than many others we have passed.

We get out and the cold evening air strikes us – a breeze from the bobbing lake that is out there somewhere in the gloom and from the wet slate hills rising mistily beyond. We listen and can hear the water slapping against the reedy shore and the wind in the trees.

I take the bags and we hurry into the well-heated hallway with its Laura Ashley wallpaper and vase full of flowers. Muddy boots are neatly lined up along the wall. The landlady is young – she looks a year or two younger than I am anyway. I don't recognize her.

'If you stayed here before we took over,' she says, in answer to my question, 'then that must be some years ago.'

'We stayed here quite often,' I say vaguely, not quite focusing on anything. 'But, yes, it was a long time ago.'

'You'll see we've made a few changes,' she says brightly. 'We don't do evening meals now though.'

'Have you kept the same room names?'

'There are some completely new rooms in the annexe, but the old ones have the same names as they did.'

'Is Skidaw free?'

'We're not too crowded at the moment.' She checks a book on the desk. 'Yes, that looks fine. It's a nice room with good views of the lake.'

'I know,' I say.

Once we are in the room, Virginia says: 'Are you sure this is a good idea?'

'It's only about ten minutes' walk into Grasmere,' I say.

'That's not what I mean. You always stayed here with your parents, right?'

'That's how I know it.'

'And this is where they were coming – the day of the accident?'

'They never got here, of course.'

'But I take it this was the room they had booked?'

'Possibly,' I say, looking round it as if there might still be clues. Pyjamas. Walking boots. Blood. 'I can't be sure. They used to book this one if they could. It's a nice room with good views of the lake and the hills. That's the sort of thing they liked.'

'Well, it's your emotional rollercoaster, I suppose, and you seem to be tall enough to be permitted to ride, but don't you think you've had enough reminders for one day? Maybe we should just stay here tonight and then find somewhere else tomorrow . . .'

'Maybe.'

I stare out of the window into the blackness. A car's headlights briefly flare up, dazzling rather than illuminating, and vanish. Until we turned off the motorway I had no plans to come here at all. I don't know why we're here rather than more conveniently located (from the point of view of tomorrow's search) in the centre of the village. I don't know what I shall feel when I wake up in this room tomorrow.

'I'm absolutely fine,' I say. 'Let's unpack and then go into the village to find somewhere to eat.'

'It's a strange coincidence,' says Virginia, 'Malcolm showing up in a place where you used to go with your parents.'

'We went to all sorts of places,' I say. What I don't add is that I thought I had an even stranger coincidence on my hands. But if Malcolm is alive then it's just a regular sort of coincidence.

'Are you sure you're OK, Puppy?' asks Virginia.

I tear myself away from thoughts of coincidences.

'I'm fine,' I repeat. 'No need to worry about good old Chris.'

* * *

That evening we drive back into Ambleside for dinner rather than take a short walk into Grasmere. Virginia says she noticed a nice restaurant as we were passing through an hour or so before. There are several nice restaurants, though it is not clear exactly which one attracted Virginia's attention. We choose one that seems as good as any of the others.

As we wait for our food to arrive, we do not talk about Malcolm Biggenhalgh. We do not talk about my work. We do not talk about Virginia's work. We do not talk about my family. We do not talk about love. We do not talk about grief. We agree there's a lot of rubbish on television. We wonder about global warming. We are not sure which is more important. All evening we skirt around the issues, then drive back towards Grasmere and an early night in a familiar room.

For a long time I lie in the bed my parents didn't get to sleep in and listen to Virginia breathing. From time to time, I hear a car pass on the road outside. Then there is nothing.

* * *

It is a particularly fine early morning in Grasmere. We have parked the car opposite Malcolm Biggenhalgh's house. It calls itself a cottage, and if that is how it thinks of itself, fine. It is, however, a fairly substantial late-Victorian house that would, in a better and kinder world, have roses flowering above the door and lavender growing in the garden. The walls are slate, like much else around here. The door is bright red and newly painted. The (also red) garden gate looks as if it will swing noiselessly on its well-oiled hinges. There are lace curtains. It's not what I was expecting. But even dashing drivers of MGs settle down eventually, I guess.

We have been here for fifteen minutes now, just sitting and watching. Soon he's going to think it's odd.

'He's going to think it's odd,' I say.

'What?' says Virginia.

'Us, just sitting here and watching his house.'

'Only if he comes out,' says Virginia. 'Then we can get a good look at him, and we'll have found out what we need to know.'

I think I see the lace curtain of the left-hand downstairs window twitch. But it is a brief movement and I am not sure. Nothing happens for a bit. Then a woman in her fifties, wearing the sort of wraparound apron that I'm sure you can no longer buy, briefly emerges on the doorstep and slowly deposits an empty milk bottle. She straightens up, looks a little too briefly in our direction, then goes back in.

'That's odd,' says Virginia. 'The milkman was delivering just as we arrived, so why put out milk bottles now?'

'We've been rumbled,' I say.

The lace curtain moves slightly again. This time I am certain. There are two vague shadows behind it. I'd put good money on one being Malcolm's.

'We can't stay here much longer,' I add. 'They'll call the police in a moment.'

'We've every right to be here. We could be checking the map or . . . or . . .'

'Quite,' I say.

Fortunately there is a cafe a few yards down the road, with a large bow window, apparently designed to give a passable view of the Biggenhalgh place, if you crane your neck a bit. We get slowly out of the car, ostentatiously consulting a map as we do so, and walk even more slowly towards the cafe, which advertises breakfast. Seated in the bow window, Virginia orders a cappuccino. I order a second breakfast to augment the large one that was provided, just half an hour before, by a guesthouse that thought we were the sort of people who ate only one breakfast a day. We sit and wait. One of us eats.

'Shit!' I say suddenly.

Virginia looks up from her coffee, spoon poised in the frothy mess at the bottom of the cup. 'What?'

'Nothing,' I say.

It's a tricky one to explain, but I have been playing the Ten People Game and have just lost. The Ten People Game works like this. You are waiting for your girlfriend, say, at the entrance to a tube station (one of the best places to play, as it happens) and are very bored. So, you assume you are obliged to sleep with one of the next ten people to come off the escalator or you will Die a Horrible Death. You are allowed to make up your own Horrible Death but it has to be pretty gruesome. The first person comes off the escalator.

It is a girl in her early twenties – not entirely unattractive but not exactly your type. You say 'no'. Having said 'no', of course, you cannot subsequently go back and say 'yes'. Having said 'yes', you can't change your mind if something better turns up and you have to check out the remaining nine people to see how much of a mistake you have made. Now you have nine choices left – that's OK. The next four to arrive, however, consist of a group of Spurs supporters on their way to the match. They are ugly even by Spurs standards. Now you are down to five choices and getting a bit worried. Next is an attractive middle-aged woman, smartly dressed. Possible? No? Yes? *No*. OK then, that's four left. Then two more Spurs supporters, racing to catch up with their mates. Two to go. The ninth is another girl in her twenties, the identical twin perhaps of the first one. So do you now opt for her, or do you wait for number ten – be it man, woman or dog? What to do?

The other name of the game is the Real Life Game, because it seems to encapsulate the sort of dilemma we suffer all the time – take one opportunity and it rules out others. Wait too long and you could end up having sex with a bunch of Spurs supporters. It happens, believe me.

'Nothing,' I say.

Virginia looks out of the bow window at the filthy old tramp shuffling past, clutching his ragged supermarket bags filled with a variety of junk. Dirt is permanently etched into every line on his face, every fold in his clothes. You can smell him just by looking at him.

Virginia turns to me. 'I sometimes wish I knew what went on in your funny little mind,' she says.

As I say, this could be a tricky one to explain, but I don't need to because I have just grasped Virginia's arm and said: 'Look – over there!'

The just visible red door of the Biggenhalgh place has opened and a man has stepped into the front garden. Is this our first view of Malcolm?

We watch as he crosses the road and inspects the fine British sports car, parked but now empty, at the kerb-side. He does not appear to be admiring the leather gearstick or even the one good wing mirror. His gaze redirects itself like tracer bullets, along the open road and towards the cafe in which we are seated. Even at this distance, I am pretty sure that that is a crooked smile on his face. Even at this distance, too, I am slightly surprised at one thing.

'He's not what I expected,' I say politely.

'You mean he's an ugly bastard, bearing in mind he's my father,' says Virginia.

'Now you mention it . . .'

'So, are you insulting my father?' demands Virginia.

'What do you want me to say? He's the spitting image of you?'

'No, thanks.'

'So why,' I ask, 'would your mother have left your dad for your father? It doesn't make sense.'

'Not put like that, anyway,' says Virginia.

Malcolm is getting closer. His walk is ponderous, as befits a man his size and age. He has pulled his tweed cap down over his eyes, though to what purpose is unclear. We are all playing a very bad game of I Spy.

'What do we do?' I ask. 'Pretend nothing is wrong or hide under the table?'

There is no time for a debate. Though there is every chance one of us will hide under the table leaving the other trying to pretend nothing is wrong, we both decide to look nonchalant. Virginia possibly succeeds. Malcolm nevertheless looks contemptuously at us as he passes. His look says that, whatever our game is, he's more than a match for us.

'The good news,' says Virginia, 'is that he merely seems to have us down as a pair of idiots.'

'So, not a good way to meet my future father-in-law?' I say. Then I realize what I've said and wonder what I meant by it.

Virginia seems not to have noticed. She is very deep in thought. 'Surely that can't be the dashing Malcolm?' she says.

'Too much like a retired hill farmer?'

'No, *precisely* like a retired hill farmer. You don't get a face like that in a merchant bank. You don't get a jacket like that anywhere inside the M25.'

'Bucolic?'

'That's the word that sums it all up.'

'What now?' I ask.

'You follow him,' she says. Then, taking stock of my likely skills, she adds: 'No, you pay the bill. I'll follow him.'

Virginia vanishes through the door as I calculate what the bill could be at its maximum, discover I only have twenties in my wallet and slap one by my plate. I wave to the girl behind the counter as I sprint away, and she waves back cautiously, just as you would to a customer who has eaten an unnecessary breakfast and then departed at a rapid pace leaving a 150 per cent tip. I probably should not go back to that cafe again.

I catch Virginia outside Read's bookshop. She has apparently lost interest in finding her lost father and is admiring the display of Lakes-related literature, which suggests a shorter attention span than I was expecting. Well, I've had enough of this if she has.

'Look natural,' she whispers to the *Complete Works of Wainwright*, artfully displayed in the window. 'He's just over there.'

'Where?' I say, looking round.

'Look at the nice books, stupid,' she hisses. 'Don't you know how to tail *any*body?'

'I understand how, I do not understand why,' I say, feeling a literary quotation is appropriate when you are hiding behind a bookshop.

'We can't suddenly tell him in front of his wife that he has a daughter. You need to take him to one side and find the appropriate words.'

'Oh, right,' I say. '*I* do that, do I? But . . .'

A couple of passing hikers, who have overheard much of the preceding conversation, give us a puzzled glance, but we ignore them.

'Quick,' says Virginia. 'He's moved on. Keep on his tail. Observe his conduct.'

We follow him through the village, using whatever cover we can. I can't quite see the point, but it is fun. And it's fun,

I reflect, mainly because I'm doing it with Virginia. We duck behind the sort of mossy stone wall that ought to have a poet leaning up against it (inconvenient though that would be for us this morning).

'Even if Malc hasn't spotted us,' I say, 'everyone else in the village has.'

'He's gone into the church,' she says, pointing in the direction of the ample lych-gate.

'It's not Sunday,' I say.

'You didn't need a second breakfast,' she says. 'That didn't stop us choosing the cafe.'

'Actually—' I say.

'No, Chris, actually you *didn't* need a second breakfast.'

'No,' I say, 'actually he hasn't gone into the church. Actually he's hiding in the churchyard, watching us watching him.'

This is true. He has ducked into the church to throw us off the scent or something. He is standing, sideways on, behind a tree, trying to be Harry Lime (or similar). Well, it's been good but the point has arrived where somebody has to act like a grown-up, and strangely it looks as if that will have to be me.

I step out from the cover of the wall and stride manfully towards the little church. As I do so I hear Virginia hiss: 'Chris!' at me, because I haven't actually discussed my plan with her. This is possibly because striding manfully is as far as I've thought this through, but it's also because if I don't do something now, I know we'll skulk around the village all day. At the same moment, Malcolm appears to have the same idea, except he strides manfully away from the church.

We meet at the lych-gate. He is blocking my way in and I am blocking his way out. One of us is going to have to speak. Inevitably, both of us do.

'What . . . hi . . . the bloody hell . . . I'm Chris, you . . . do you two young idiots . . . don't know me but . . . think you're playing at . . . I'm going out with your daughter,' we say in close harmony.

'You what?' he says solo, having picked up the last few words and discovered it was all a bit more exciting than he thought.

'I think I said: Hi, I'm Chris, you don't know me but I'm going out with your daughter.'

Should I take the opportunity to ask him for her hand in marriage? Probably a bit forward on my part. I therefore smile in a friendly manner and allow him a moment or two for the other information to sink in.

'I don't have a daughter,' he says, in much the same way that you might say: 'Honestly, officer, I had no idea that it was a forty-mile-an-hour-speed limit here.'

'Think back a bit,' I suggest helpfully.

He pauses and thinks.

'Is that her?' He looks in the direction of Virginia, who has also chosen to emerge from her hiding place, and is now looking at us both with evident incredulity.

'Yes,' I say.

'Bugger,' he says. He doesn't add anything about it being a fair cop, but clearly it is.

'She'd like to meet you.'

'Is her mother here as well?'

'No, she's in Horsham.'

He raises his bushy eyebrows. 'Horsham, eh?'

I nod.

'We can't talk here,' he says, ignoring the fact that we already are. 'Meet me in Ambleside, the both of you.' He names a cafe and a time. I nod again.

'When you pick up that wreck of a car, don't do anything to make my wife suspicious.'

I don't tell him I've spent the morning making half of Grasmere suspicious. I figure he'll find out soon enough.

He looks around cautiously to see who might have seen us and, touchingly reassured, he sets off without a further word. I go in the opposite direction and rejoin Virginia.

'And?' she asks.

'He knows he has a daughter. He is relieved your mother is in Horsham. He wants to meet us in Ambleside.'

'And if I don't want to meet him?'

'But you do,' I point out.

(Pause.)

'He seems OK,' I add. 'Not what I expected, but OK.'

(Long pause.)

'Fine,' she says.

15

A Touching Reunion in Ambleside

Malcolm has named eleven thirty as the proper hour for us to meet, so we have a certain amount of time to kill. We check out the Wordsworth tombstones in the churchyard (William, Dorothy, etc., still all present and correct, plus some that I've never heard of and that I think they may have made up). We admire the Wordsworth Daffodil Gardens, albeit without daffodils at this time of year. We wonder who could have thought it was a good idea to pebbledash the church. Then we stroll slowly back to the car, get in very quickly, and drive to Ambleside.

We park expensively and wander aimlessly around different streets, looking in shop windows at various things we might wish to purchase to remind us of our visit, just in case we are likely to forget. For the first thirty to forty seconds, it is fun.

'Why did he say eleven thirty?' asks Virginia for the tenth time. 'It doesn't take that long to get here.'

'He didn't say.'

'You could have asked him.'

I don't reply. Virginia is building up to a Number Seventeen (vague but persistent irritation concerning something I haven't done that I had no reason to suspect I needed to do).

'You could have asked him,' says Virginia again.

'Yes,' I say.

'God, you're an idiot.'

'Probably, but thank you—'

She gives me a look and I don't complete the sentence. I have been demoted from being a beloved Puppy and am back to being the Idiot Chris, a role that I am at least familiar with and quite good at. I wonder whether I might not, after all, think of a pet name for her. I am no longer sure that I do want to dump her. Perhaps it might be nice to spend the rest of my life playing detectives with her, if we can just get our act together in that respect.

Our aimless wanderings have brought us to a jeweller's shop. We pause as we have paused outside so many shops already and admire the bracelets, the necklaces and the rings.

'That solitaire diamond must cost a bit,' I say to fill in some time.

'I'd want one bigger than that,' says Virginia, and gives my hand a squeeze.

Oh, my God! Have I just accidentally got engaged? I pull myself together. This is the twenty-first century, not the days of Mr Pickwick and Mrs Bardell.

But actually, there are worse potential outcomes of this

little trip than to return and tell Daphne that she shall be blessed with a son-in-law and that his name shall be called Chris. I sneak a look at the rather attractive girl beside me and think that, her regarding me as an imbecile apart, I am actually quite lucky. If I went down on one knee now she would almost certainly assume it was some sort of mistimed joke, but in many other respects it seems a good move.

We stay looking at the rings longer than we looked at the displays of Kendal Mint Cake or twee model houses or Beatrix Potter-related gifts. We are still holding hands as we move on, edging slowly towards our meeting with Malcolm.

Inevitably we are at the cafe first and order more coffees while we sit and wait. When he does arrive, we receive a further surprise. He is dressed in a smart suit, a white shirt and a very new lilac silk tie. His grey hair, relieved of the tweed cap, is manfully combed and possibly Brylcreemed.

He spots us and walks purposefully in our direction, barging into one of two occupied chairs as he does. He gives the briefest of apologies to each before dropping heavily into the unoccupied seat at our table.

'Had to tell the wife I was off to see the bank manager,' he says, by way of introduction.

He looks approvingly at Virginia. Virginia looks at him and smiles. If he wasn't won over already, that's the smile that will do it. I wish that I had brought a camera to record this. I'd like to be able to freeze the moment for them – to allow them to enjoy it for ever. Particularly since their enjoyment is in fact destined to be short.

'So,' says Malcolm after a long pause, 'you're my daughter then. I always suspected something of the sort, but she never told me a thing. Not a thing. Just upped and off. So, she's in Horsham now?'

'That's right,' says Virginia.

He shakes his head. 'Horsham, eh? Really?'

'Yes, of course. I thought you knew that. Ever since she married Hugh, pretty much.'

'Hugh?' says Malcolm.

Virginia looks a little puzzled. 'Yes, of course,' she says again.

Malcolm repeats the head-shaking thing, then gets back onto what he thinks is firmer ground. 'Well, well,' he says. 'So, you're Betty's little girl, eh?' He smiles.

'Betty?' says Virginia.

Now, I don't know whether you have been following the conversation as you should, but if you have then you will have noticed the merest hint that all is not well.

'Your mother, Betty,' says Malcolm, still slightly off the pace.

'You mean Daphne,' says Virginia.

'I mean Betty.'

'I know what my mother's called.'

'Never had a Daphne,' he announces. 'Never shall, neither.'

'Look . . .' I say.

Malcolm turns to me abruptly. 'I thought you said this were Betty's girl,' he demands.

'I said she was your daughter,' I said.

'You said Betty lived in Horsham.'

'I said her mother lived in Horsham.'

'Well, bugger me,' he observes to nobody in particular. 'I've put on my best suit to come and have coffee with a pair of total strangers. What exactly are you playing at, young man?' This last remark is addressed directly at me.

'Good question,' says Virginia with a nod.

They are both looking at me in a curious manner, though I am still trying to work out how this is my fault. It seems to me that we have all been jumping to conclusions, and that mine have been no worse than anyone else's. Or not much.

'Wait a minute,' I say. 'Her father's name *is* Malcolm Biggenhalgh. It's not exactly the most common name in England. You might still be able to help us . . .'

'Happen I could and happen I couldn't,' he says slowly, 'but I'll tell you now, I won't. I don't like being made to look a fool. You've wasted enough of my time, so I'll bid you both good day.'

He stands up. Virginia is still looking at him through narrowed eyes.

'Are you sure you won't help us?'

'I'm certain of it,' he says.

'Even though we know about Betty and know where you live?'

'We know you've got a terrier called Scruff,' I add.

They both look at me again with a sort of sad curiosity. I am clearly a total failure as a blackmailer.

'It's obviously not Scruff we're planning to talk to,' says Virginia, getting things back on track.

Malcolm sits down again.

'I'll have one of those vanilla latte things,' he says, 'and I can't stay more than ten minutes. Now, what do you want to know?'

I wave ineffectively at passing waitresses (who clearly do not know that I leave 150 per cent tips) while Virginia focuses on the questions.

'Are there lots of other Biggenhalghs round here?'

'Depends what you call lots,' says Malcolm. 'There's my brother John, who farms over by Windermere, and my brother Ken, who's an auctioneer in Keswick. They've both got grown-up kids and even a grandchild, but no Malcolms. I've got a cousin Tom, who lives near Newcastle, and a cousin Ray, who died a couple of years back. No Malcolms there either.' He shrugs: we've played our best card and it's got us nowhere.

'Anyone else?' Virginia is more persistent than I expected.

'There are a couple of gravestones in Keswick with our name on, but I don't know they're any sort of kin.' He covers the family a few generations back, just to show he has nothing to hide, by which time the coffees arrive.

'The problem is,' he concludes, stirring in outsized amounts of sugar, 'when you're called Malcolm Biggenhalgh, you tend to remember if you run into anyone else called Malcolm Biggenhalgh. That's why I don't think I'm going to be much use to you.' We drink our coffees almost in silence, then Malcolm checks his watch, stands up again and says: 'Look, if I think of owt else, I'll phone you.'

We give him mobile numbers but without much hope that they will be of use to him.

When he has gone, Virginia gives a little giggle: '"I've never had a Daphne and never shall neither." I can't wait to tell my mother that one.'

'Sorry,' I say.

'Don't be. We had to find out. If we hadn't spoken to him, I might have spent the rest of my life believing he was my father. I'm sure he's a nice man, but not at all my mother's type. As for fathers, I'm not sure I know what my type is any more, but probably not him. A bit humourless, wouldn't you say? So, we're no further forward and no further back than we were.'

We find an Internet cafe, where I check my emails. Virginia says she'll phone her office and wanders outside into the sunshine. I log on with trepidation.

The first thing is an email from Jon.

Chris – I hope you're picking up emails, wherever you are. We've got problems. Digby Spain phoned asking for more information about George Magwitch. When I refused, he said the Society had already set him up with an interview, so what was the problem now? He said he could get hold of GM anyway and rung off. I went storming into Roger's office to accuse him of interfering and, obviously, told him all I know. He said he hadn't spoken to DS but he looked a bit worried all the same. I need to know if either of you have had contact with DS so I can try to repair the damage. Pl phone or email soonest. J

Next, Humph:

Dear Chris,

I would be much obliged if you could give me a call at your very earliest convenience re Spain. Yours ever, Roger.

One from Lucy. (Excellent.):

Chris

If you were not going to turn up, you might have at least phoned. How difficult exactly would that have been? And where are you now? Have fun, but don't hurry back on my account. Lucy

Another from Jon:

Chris – it's hotting up. A contact in the press office at RCP phoned to warn me that Digby Spain is planning to shaft Magwitch in Thursday's edition. Don't know how he knows. Roger is really pissed off. Can you tell me anything? For God's sake, email me, text me, phone me. J

And from George Magwitch:

Dear Chris,

Roger phoned me to say that this Spain chap might be a bit unreliable. I reassured him that Spain was your choice and that I trusted you 100 per cent. I have had a second chat with him now and I rather think Spain is sound and will do the business for us. If you get a chance, though, phone me. I have one or two interesting bits of info that I don't want to put into one of these email things.

Yours till the chickens come home to roost,

George

Professor George Magwitch

University of Devon Medical School

And from Dave

Southend v Colchester Saturday. Roots Hall. Are you up for it? Dave.

And from Barbara Proudie:

Christian

This time we've got him!!!! We've been talking to Digby Spain and on Thursday he is going to tell the truth about Dan Smith – and about George Magwitch and his so-called research. I've also told Digby about the number of times I've asked your Society to take action and that you've done nothing at all. Nothing, Christian. You'll be losing your Royal Charter and don't say I haven't warned you over and over again but do you listen? You've nobody else to blame but yourselves. Now you'll see the truth of what I've been telling you all this time. You had your chance, Christian, and now the Society is going down with George Magwitch. It will be no loss.

Barbara

And from Jon again:

Chris – Roger is fuming but won't tell me anything. Please, please ring me. J

'Still at it?' asks Virginia, returning from the fresh sunny lands beyond the cafe door. She is smiling. Something has pleased her immensely.

'You look happy,' I say.

'Do I? I hadn't intended to. Somebody at work must have said something to amuse me.'

'Nobody at work had any jokes for me.'

'Bad luck. So, how are things back at base?'

'Couldn't be better,' I say, logging off. 'Fancy a walk up Easedale after lunch?'

16

Easedale, 5 May this Year

It's not a good time of year for people who don't like blossom. The bush-packed cottage gardens and the flat, improbably green fields are full of apple blossom, pear blossom, horse chestnut blossom, cherry blossom, May blossom. Rich cream, bridal white, baby pink, pastel blue and soft ephemeral yellow are all there somewhere. Everything says: 'Rejoice! The winter is over.' You have to go high up into the fells to escape the insistent colour, up into the lumpy brownness of the dead fern, where the odd purple-blue flower, peeping out shyly from the damp moss, can be trodden kindly but firmly under your size nine boot. It may be spring in the valley, but up here you know the glaciers could be back any time they choose. It's a reassuring place for pessimists to be.

We have parked in Grasmere (but at a considerate distance from Malcolm's place and far from any restaurants where I might recently have embarrassed myself). Then we have headed for the hills. The valley floor was full of white-faced sheep conscientiously nibbling the spring shoots. They seemed cautiously happy on the whole, as sheep do. Down there everything smells of shit, but in a good way.

We picked our path on a whim and followed a beck that was so clear it seemed to have no depth at all. Much higher up we could see the same stream as it pitched over the grey rocks in thin, apparently motionless, snowy threads. This illusion appeared to offer us a frozen and silent realm. It seemed the right way to go.

Now we are up by the same waterfall, and the cascade is no longer a distant and soundless blemish on the rocks but an immediate and powerful rush of icy water that threatens to suck you in if you stare too long at it. We stare for as long as seems safe. Then there is another half a mile or so of easy walking and we finally find ourselves seated on a rough sandstone boulder looking across the tarn and towards the grim arc of hills behind. The hills seem close until you look at the bright little specks of hill-walking humanity working their way slowly up the track that slants lazily across them. A no-nonsense northern breeze is blowing across the tarn. Although the sun is shining, it is cold enough to remind you that summer never gains more than a toehold at this altitude.

'It's strange,' I say, 'the way water looks like everything except water. It's all reflection. That tarn looks a bit like the sky, a bit like the hills behind it. Even the ripples you can see are more about the wind than the water itself.'

'Whatever you say, Puppy,' says Virginia, as she does when I'm talking crap. Her mind is on other things. Only mine is free to roam (a bit like that Wordsworth's, really) gathering images that I shall file away.

'Still thinking about Malcolm?' This is a pretty safe guess on my part.

'Wherever he is.'

'We'll find him,' I say.

Virginia shifts her weight slightly. It's not the softest of rocks we are sitting on and Virginia (in spite of what she fears) does not have a vast amount of natural padding. Her eyes take in the hills, the dots making their slow way diagonally up to the col, and the smooth sweep of the tarn, broken only by a solitary rock that barely raises its head above the surface several hundred yards out. Somewhere in the distance a dog barks, then there is just the sound of water lapping the shingle below us.

'At least this is solid and real,' she says.

'Do you think so?' I say.

'Obviously.'

'Has it never occurred to you that this might all be in your imagination?'

'No,' says Virginia. 'I bet it's occurred to you though.'

'Yes,' I say.

'What's that like then, living in your own imaginary world?'

'On the plus side, all this belongs to me. On the minus side, I've got nobody to whom I can brag about it.'

'You know, Chris, I sometimes think your mind must be a bit like a join-up-the-dots-puzzle but without the numbers.'

I nod. She's right. It is a bit like that.

'But why shouldn't all this exist?' asks Virginia.

This is, of course, a tricky one to explain. I summarize Cartesian Dualism in a few well-chosen sentences, but the ideas seem strangely small set against the irrefutable massiveness of the fells. Virginia is not convinced.

'So, Descartes starts by suggesting that everything might be imagined, but concludes that it is real after all?'

'Because God wouldn't lie to him.'

'But he can only be certain of God's existence because he is certain of the reality that God has just endorsed?'

'More or less. It's the Cartesian Circle – a sort of merry-go-round for philosophers. You can play on it as long as you like.'

'So he doesn't prove God exists?'

'He thought he did. The only real proof of God's existence is, however, Fat Dave's.'

'Fat Dave's?'

'That's right. I'll summarize it for you.'

17

Fat Dave's Proof of the Existence of God

Look, Chris, it's like this. [Burp.]

There are only two mutually exclusive possibilities. God exists or God does not exist. Right?

Let's take the possibility that God does *not* exist. If that's the case, then what do we have? The solar system is a minute speck in the universe and our sun is an almost invisible pinpoint of light in the middle of it. Round this pinpoint of light a completely irrelevant speck of dust rotates once every 365 days. Living on this irrelevant speck of dust are these nearly invisible micro-specks, which survive as a race for approximately one blink of the celestial eye. Nothing that happens to the irrelevant speck can possibly count for anything and the micro-specks are, individually and collectively, so unimportant to the universe that nothing they could do would make the slightest difference, even during the brief flicker of an eyelid that is allotted to them. Logically, therefore, it does not matter if we treat each other well or badly. The very best we can do, the worst we can do, is all over in a flash and the universe is unchanged. Logically it does not matter if we steal, kill, rape, set up concentration camps, park on double yellow lines or support Colchester United. [Burp. Significant pause.]

Why then does every known society believe in the rightness of a morality that goes beyond tactics for survival – that is to say, beyond a policy of 'I won't do it to you if you won't do it to me'? Why do we think it's commendable to help other people, even if there's nothing in it for us? Why do we believe that anything matters beyond the simple enjoyment of what we can lay our hands on?

The fact that we do believe in a just and moral world, in spite of overwhelming logical arguments for pure self-interest, is the proof that God exists. I can't tell you whether he eats bacon sandwiches, or whether he actually likes you that much, but he's out there somewhere.

If you get your round in now, it will be proof that there are also miracles, but in the meantime we can at least be sure there is a God.

18

Easedale, 5 May this Year

'It's original,' says Virginia.

'Not really,' I say. 'Kant said something similar. So did Sartre.'

'Didn't Kant say that God was dead?'

'That was Nietzsche. Fat Dave says that God can hear the phone ringing but can't be arsed to pick up. It's the sort of deity Fat Dave can relate to.'

'Why do you call him Fat Dave?' asks Virginia.

'Because he's fat?'

'No, he's not. If anything I'd say you were carrying a few more surplus pounds than David.'

'I don't look as though I work out at the gym?'

'Your flat is on top of the gym. Working out at the gym and living over it are not the same thing, Chris.'

'He used to be fat at school,' I say. 'Well, plump anyway. Nicknames stick. Once a fat bastard, always a fat bastard in my book.'

'Do you imagine,' says Virginia, 'that if you are gratuitously rude about your friends other people will like you better?'

Now, even I realize that the correct answer to this question is not an enthusiastic and unqualified 'yes'. It's just that I'd never really thought about it in those terms. Obviously I am rude about Dave because he is a mate. That's how things are. As far as I can see, I'm no ruder about other people than they deserve.

'You and Dave are not good influences on each other,' she continues.

This too is a new one. Dave is clearly a bad influence on me – that's what I like about him – but I can't see how I am a bad influence on him. I point this out.

'No,' says Virginia. 'You are both reasonably normal alone. It's when you get together that you both cease to resemble educated adult human beings.'

I say nothing.

'I mean,' she continues, 'you seem to have only three topics of conversation.'

I think about this. Sex and football, obviously. What's the third one? We did discuss Nietzsche the other day, but I'd scarcely admit that to anyone.

'Three?' I say.

She looks at me pityingly. 'I thought I'd give you the benefit of the doubt.' She stands up. 'Time to go back down.'

I pick up the rucksack. 'Then down we go,' I say.

* * *

We have not gone far when my mobile phone rings. It makes me jump because I've had it switched off for the past couple of days, not wishing to know if Lucy or Humph or Jon is on my case. I wouldn't say ignorance is bliss exactly, but it's actually not that bad.

Virginia is for some reason a little way ahead of me – far enough ahead that, if this is Lucy, I could do the decent thing, take the call and face up to my responsibilities. (As if.) I check the screen cautiously. It's not Lucy or Humph or any other number I recognize. I press the button decisively and take the call.

'It's Malcolm,' my phone announces, and for a moment I think Virginia's father has miraculously found us. Then I realize it is not the real thing but the bucolic pseudo-father.

'Hi,' I say.

'I won't beat about the bush,' he says. 'That's not my way. But I've just remembered something.'

'Ah . . .' I say.

'Is that young lass of yours with you?'

'We're walking back down Easedale. She's a bit ahead of me. I'll call her.'

'No, no,' he says urgently. 'It's you I want to talk to.'

'Ah . . .' I say again.

'You remember I said I couldn't think of anyone else called Malcolm Biggenhalgh?'

'Yes.'

'Well, maybe I do after all. I was thinking back. It was at Ray's funeral – Ray my second cousin. There was somebody there I didn't recognize. That's how it is at funerals – all sorts of people you know quite well plus a few distant relatives you see once in a blue moon plus one or two others you don't know from Adam.'

I agree that funerals are a bit like that, but I can't quite see where this is going.

'So was there another Malcolm at the funeral . . .?'

'Not Malcolm – Martin. Young chap – about twenty or so then. I'd never set eyes on him before. I can't remember how he was related to Ray or to me, but his name was Martin Biggenhalgh.'

'Still not with you, Malcolm,' I say. For somebody who did not beat about the bush he is at least having a darned good try.

'One or two people there were talking to him about his father – Mally, they called him. Mally – short for Malcolm, do you see? Didn't really register on me at the time – his father's name and mine being the same. They all kept saying Mally.'

'Ah . . .' I say for a third time. I wonder whether to tell him that Mally, having the same number of syllables as Malcolm, can't be short for anything. But I just say: 'And where does Mally live?'

'Well,' says Malcolm, 'that's the point. They were all asking how Martin and his mother were getting on since his father died.'

'So, the other Malcolm – our Malcolm – is dead: that's what you're saying?'

'Seems like it,' he says. 'Maybe it's best if you break the news to the young lass.'

'Maybe,' I say. I am trying to gain a bit of time and think this through, because I don't really want to break the news to Virginia that she is an orphan all over again.

Malcolm is saying his goodbyes and about to ring off when I say: 'Hang on, where does *Martin* live?'

'Horsham,' he says. 'He told me he lived in Horsham. Small world, eh?'

* * *

I have, for all sorts of reasons, been walking slowly, and it is not until Virginia stops that I catch her up.

'Come on, slowcoach,' she says cheerfully. She smiles and I suddenly realize that I have the power to make her very unhappy and that I cannot decently avoid doing it.

I check that there is nobody approaching us on the path and likely to overhear us before I say: 'That was Malcolm from Grasmere.'

'What did he want?'

'He'd remembered something. Look, do you want to sit down?'

'Why should I want to do that?'

I nod. I figure she's not going to keel over like some pale Victorian heroine, though sitting still seems quite a good plan. I check there's a rock nearby.

'Malcolm says he does remember another Malcolm Biggenhalgh, but that he died some time back. I'm sorry. I'm really sorry.'

I explain about Martin and everything. For a moment she says nothing. Then it's her turn to cry and my turn to be the strong one with a firm but absorbent shoulder. I'm glad I chose a spot where nobody was about to overtake or pass us. I offer her a nice rock, but she prefers to cling onto me a bit longer.

'Thank you,' she says after a bit. 'Thank you for telling me straight away.'

'It might not be your father,' I say.

'Oh, come on . . . how many Malcolm Biggenhalghs are there going to be? And his son lives in Horsham.'

I pass her a tissue, which I have in the rucksack and which is, surprisingly, quite clean. She blows her nose. I take back the tissue and put it in my pocket. There aren't many people whose snotty tissue I would willingly carry around with me.

'You know,' I say, 'I'd do anything for you. Anything at all.'

'Yes, I know,' she says, watching me pocket the tissue. She takes my hand and does not let go until we are safely back in sheep land.

I am walking through a green valley with spring blossom everywhere. At my side is the person with whom I wish to spend the rest of my life. All I need to do is to find a way of telling her that does not sound like one of my one-liners. And sooner or later I shall find a way of doing this.

The sheep turn their attention briefly from the grass and look at us as if they have always known we would be back sooner or later. Smug bastards. They'd be a bit less cocky if they realized that they didn't exist.

* * *

We are back at the guesthouse for our final evening in Grasmere. I have been sitting at the desk for some time writing on a sheet of A4 paper.

'What's that?' asks Virginia after a bit, breaking my train of thought.

I hand the sheet to her. It reads:

> <u>On Stopping in a Bar on a Snowy Evening</u>
> *It's getting very late I know*
> *And really now I ought to go*
> *But still there's time for one more beer*
> *Before I face the rain and snow.*
>
> *My wife must think it rather queer*
> *That dinner's done and I'm still here*
> *Instead of eating pasta bake*
> *With those I hold most close and dear.*
>
> *She'll give her pretty head a shake*
> *Well knowing there is no mistake . . .*

'It stops in mid-verse,' she says.

'That's what happens when you start porlocking,' I say.

'It's not exactly "Kubla Khan",' she says.

'You don't like it?'

'I like the original.'

'Robert Frost,' I say. '"*On Stopping by Woods on a Snowy Evening*". The construction is brilliant. In a poem about nostalgia, the main rhyme of each stanza harks back to the unrhymed line in the stanza before.'

'Whereas in yours . . .'

I shrug. I don't believe I've ever claimed to be America's greatest twentieth-century poet. And I don't do nostalgia. Ever.

'Why do you only write pastiches?' she asks. 'You could do so much better by just being you.'

I shrug again, because I don't know the answer.

'It's also very domestic for somebody who doesn't show the slightest interest in permanent relationships.' She raises an eyebrow.

Is this the moment? What could lead more easily into a proposal? What have we to fear except fear itself?

'I'm starving,' I say. 'Let's go and eat.'

I have booked a table at a small restaurant called the Jumble Room, where I've been told the food is good. Virginia surprises me by saying that she's eaten there before.

'I didn't know you'd been to Grasmere before.'

'I was just passing through. You don't know everything about me.'

I reflect that, actually, I do know pretty well everything about her by now, but I just smile and nod because I don't want an argument. Anyway, it's as well we should both save up a few bombshells like that one to while away the long winter evenings together.

When we get to the Jumble Room, Virginia is greeted as a long-lost friend. It isn't clear whether it's because she was a big hit last time or whether it's just that sort of place – which it looks as though it might be. It suddenly strikes me though that people do instinctively like Virginia: both the snotty kid on the beach and Malcolm (the almost-father) took to her like a shot. She genuinely cares about humans in a way that I need to study and see if I can fake.

We chat for a bit over the menu and the conversation turns, as in my experience it so often does, to Bishop George Berkeley (1685–1753).

'Berkeley held,' I say, 'that things existed only if perceived. *Esse est percipi*, as they say. It's the question of the tree that falls in a deserted forest with nobody to hear it fall – does it make a noise?'

'Yes,' says Virginia. 'Obviously it does, because falling trees do. You'd probably hear it for miles, whether you were in the forest or not. The lamb was good last time. I might try it again. All of the puddings are good, so don't pig yourself on the main course, as you are probably planning to. You'd like the bread-and-butter pudding.'

'Or,' I continue, 'if there is nobody in the quadrangle to see a tree, does it continue to exist?'

'Forgive me for saying this, but was Bishop Berkeley a bit tree fixated?'

'His point was that the reality of objects consists of their being perceived. He doesn't necessarily deny the existence of material things, but holds that they exist only in the mind. Logically, if you leave a room, everything in it ceases to exist until you return and perceive it again.'

'He sounds like the sort of person who is always losing his keys,' says Virginia. 'Typical man. Are you ready to order?'

We are well into our main course before we get to the big question of the evening.

'What next?' I ask.

'Pudding, I should imagine. Just concentrate on one course at a time.'

'No, I mean – finding Malcolm. Is that it? Case solved?'

'I've been thinking about that. I'd like to talk to Martin

at least. Even if Malcolm is dead, I'd like to find out something about him. Or maybe he's not the right Malcolm either, in which case I need to know, so I can have one more shot at finding him.'

'Martin it is, then,' I say. 'But, please, can we just phone him up this time, not shadow him all the way round Horsham before confronting him outside Pizza Hut.'

'That is a better plan,' she concedes.

There is a gap in the conversation during which I wonder whether *this* is in fact the moment to ask Virginia to do me the signal honour and so on and so on . . . but the waiter pauses to ask if we are enjoying our meal and, as we reflect on the quality of the battered cod, the moment somehow passes. There'll be plenty of better opportunities anyway.

* * *

There is in fact an opportunity as we walk back along the lake with the moon flickering on its deep and largely untroubled waters, but again more pressing business raises its head.

'I was wondering,' says Virginia, 'whether you would like to say a few words about Hugh at the funeral. I think it would be appropriate.'

'I'd be honoured,' is all I reply.

And so the rest of the way back I am thinking about what I should say. He was a good man. No doubt about that. A genuine friend. Honest, obviously. But behind that mild don't-mind-me exterior there was something much firmer. I remember one time when we were walking along a country lane somewhere in Sussex and came across a kitten that had just been run over. When I saw that, bloody and mangled though it was, it was still alive and wriggling, my first reaction was to throw up in the nearest bush, but Hugh just waved the rest of us on our way and stayed with it. He rejoined us after a bit. I noticed there was a bit of blood on his shoe, and thought that there must have been more that he had wiped off. Hugh was always very particular about his shoes. 'What did you do?' I asked. 'The only thing I could do,' he said. 'It wasn't going to survive, so it was better that it was over quickly.' I decided I had enough detail already, so I never discovered precisely what he had done back there in the lane, or where he had learned to give the *coup de grace* to small felines, but I was certain that whatever had been done had been efficient and right. There was a steely resolve to his compassion, whereas mine was just mushy and contemptible. I had to admire that, though it frightened me a bit too. It was a side of Hugh that I had never seen before and I wondered at the time what else he might be capable of, if push came to shove. If you can kill a kitten, then you can do a lot of other stuff – in my opinion anyway. Did it give some insight as to why such a mild-seeming man could also be so interested in bloody battles and military equipment?

I'm not sure how much of this I will be able to weave into a valedictory address – maybe not the kitten story in its full glory – but hopefully I could show that there was more to Hugh than you saw at first sight.

I was soon to discover that I had still only scratched the surface with Hugh – but, that evening, as I thought of all these things, for the third time I let slip a chance to mention to Virginia that I was planning to marry her. It didn't seem important. I rather imagined, as you do, that the moon would always be shining on Grasmere.

19

On the Road Again

We're driving south. I'm at the wheel and don't need to hand over to anybody as we pass the crash site. I'm fine. This time I have used directory enquiries and phoned ahead. Martin Biggenhalgh is bemused by my call, but willing to see us this evening. All we need to do is stop off in London again for a change of socks and maybe underwear, then onwards to Horsham.

In Islington I pull out once again the file that I have so carefully hidden away. The important paper for today's meeting is a small supplementary press cutting. I double-check. I wouldn't want to get any of this wrong.

* * *

Martin's house is almost identical to Hugh and Daphne's. There are lavender bushes growing in the garden rather than roses, and the door is green, but it might be at the other end of the same road rather than on the other side of town, as it is.

Martin opens the door. I do not doubt for one moment

that we have struck gold this time. To the extent that I can judge, as another bloke, I would say he was pretty good-looking. If father was anything like son, you can see why Daphne might just have preferred Malcolm to Hugh. Like Virginia, his features are fine and even and his eyes have the same hard, sapphire sparkle. His hair is dark and flops slightly into his eyes. He brushes it back and grins at us. The gesture and the smile are both Virginia's.

So, he looks like Virginia's brother all right. I'm convinced even if they are not. But the same thought seems to occur to Martin and Virginia. They don't for the moment ask any questions; they just say a brief 'hi' and look at each other. Based on this opening exchange, I reflect that Martin would also probably sound just like Virginia's brother if it were not for the hint of a Newcastle accent. It's a strange moment, and I feel like an intruder. But I'm not an intruder. In my own small way, I'm part of this evening's discussion too. They just don't know it yet.

Martin ushers us both into the sitting room.

'My wife is putting the children to bed,' he says. 'She said she'll join us later, but . . . sorry, this is really weird. So you're my sister?'

'Half-sister, I guess,' says Virginia. 'Apparently your father was also my father, though we're not sure whether he knew it.'

Martin takes a deep breath and lets it out again. 'This is taking some getting used to. You know my father – our father – died some years ago? And my mother died last year. I didn't think I had any close family left, though I've lots of cousins and things up north. How odd that we've both been living in Horsham all this time and never knew. I bet we've passed each other dozens of times in the street.'

'So, you've been in Horsham some time?' I ask conversationally.

'We moved here from Newcastle shortly after my father died. He'd always talked of coming here for some reason. I've no idea why, except he had lived in London for a while, years back. Just before he died he'd been down to Horsham and found a house – this one actually. He passed away before the contract could be signed but we bought it and we came here anyway.'

'Not a good time to try to find that sort of money – just after you've lost a husband?' I say.

Martin smiles. 'Dad was in insurance for a long time,' he says. 'My mother was better off with him dead than with him alive. He saw to that.'

'Still, you'd have thought it would have been better to stay put,' I say.

Martin shrugs. 'I don't know why he wanted to move at all. We were perfectly happy in Newcastle. He had no problem in finding work. The move was horrendous at first. You think of Horsham as pretty law-abiding, but during our first couple of months here we had three or four break-ins. I don't think they stole much, but they made quite a mess the very last time it happened and my mother was really rattled. I thought maybe we'd be moving back to Newcastle, but then things got better and we stayed, as you can see.'

'Did he ever mention my . . . did Malcolm ever mention Hugh Dewey?' asks Virginia.

'Hugh Dewey? Yes,' says Martin. 'He was . . .'

'The man my mother married. He was the man I thought was my father.'

'This is getting weirder and weirder,' says Martin. 'Yes, I remember my parents talking about him. He was the guy who used to send us money. I wasn't supposed to know, but from time to time I'd overhear them talking. They'd say things like: "Maybe we could get Hugh Dewey to pay for it," or: "Let's hope we get Hugh's cheque before Christmas," that sort of thing. I asked my mother once who Hugh Dewey was, it must have been just after we moved here. I'd assumed he was a bit like Father Christmas, but delivered 24/7. That's why I thought she'd be happy to talk about him, but I really got a mouthful from her. As I say, she was a bit tense with all the trouble we were having with the break-ins. I never asked again – not even when I was grown up.'

I scratch my head. 'I can see why Malcolm might feel obliged to support you if he knew you were his daughter,' I say to Virginia, 'but I can't see why it should work the other way round and why Hugh should send money to Malcolm. What for?'

'People send money because they want to or because they have to,' says Virginia. 'I can't see why Hugh would want to.'

'My father wasn't the sort of person to resort to black-mail,' says Martin, nettled slightly by this suggestion.

'*Our* father,' says Virginia. 'My mother implied that Hugh sacked Malcolm from his job in London. Could that have anything to do with it?'

Martin shrugs. 'I don't remember him saying anything about that. I know he'd worked for an insurance company in

'I'm sorry,' says Martin, though it is not clear for which (if any) aspects of my life he feels personally responsible.

'It's not your fault,' I say. I turn to Virginia. 'I'd really hoped it was some other Malcolm Biggenhalgh. As long as we thought he was alive, it *had* to be some other Malcolm Biggenhalgh. Conversely, once I knew he was dead . . .' There's a further silence during which I add philosophically: 'It's a funny old world.' Everyone nods because, actually, it is.

'My father should never have been there at all,' says Martin. 'He'd been working too many shifts as it was. He agreed to do that one at the last minute . . .'

Martin's wife chooses this moment to appear at the door. We all turn and look at her. She is clearly unsure of the etiquette for being introduced to your late father-in-law's love child. She smiles sweetly at each of us in turn.

'Well,' she says brightly, 'I should think you must all be ready for a nice cup of tea?'

I nod and, at the same time, realize that I have again told the story of the crash without mentioning Neils in any way. I wonder exactly what will be needed to happen to make that thing possible. Maybe if I just told everyone now, very, very quickly and without thinking about it in advance?

'Ah yes, tea,' I say. 'I'd love some tea.'

20

London, 1752

The Hostess moved through the crowded room, bearing a delicate porcelain cup in her small white hand. Her eyes tracked the progress of a footman carrying a teapot, followed closely by a maid who was carefully holding a silver tray on which were sugar, milk and a tea-strainer. Observing that all was as it should be, at least for the moment, she pressed on to the far side of the room where one of her guests sat alone, though his bulk made him as prominent as any object in the room. Mr (not yet Dr) Johnson had placed himself defiantly in a large armchair, daring any of those assembled to speak to him. The Hostess smiled sweetly.

'Mr Johnson, is there nobody here worthy of your attention?'

'Madam, there are many here who are worthy of my attention, but I am worthy of nobody's. I have brought the black dog with me on its leash and it sits here snarling.'

The Hostess looked to the left and right of Mr Johnson's chair to confirm that the dog in question was metaphorical rather than material.

would know if they read any of my books *with care*. I do not deny the reality of that which is perceived by our senses, but we do not see the *causes* of colours or hear the *causes* of sounds. We see colours and we hear sounds, which are merely qualities of the things themselves. Things exist only to the extent that we perceive them to exist. *Esse est percipi.*'

'So, it's all in my mind?'

'Take heat,' said Berkeley, sidestepping the grubby contents of a lexicographer's mind. 'Now, as you know, if you put your right hand in cold water and the left one in hot water then place them both in tepid water, the water will feel hot to the right hand and cold to the left. But the water cannot be hot and cold simultaneously. The water is neither hot nor cold except that you perceive it to be so.'

'So, sir, the existence of an unperceived object is an impossibility.'

'In theory, yes.'

'Very well, sir, I may perceive the tiles on the roof of a church, but not the beams that hold them in place. By your reckoning the tiles should then come crashing down because the beams do not exist.'

'God sees the beams,' said Berkeley, 'so they continue to hold His roof up.'

'And the roof of a house of ill-repute?'

'God is omnipresent.'

'Rarely,' said Johnson, 'have I heard such nonsense.'

'There are those that I would recognize as great men, and I hope whom you would recognize as great men, whose writings would support my contentions.'

'It is the fate of great men, sir, to have their persons and their ideas ludicrously caricatured by lesser writers who come after them. It may happen to us too. But as for your theory of the non-existence of matter, I refute it thus.' Johnson lashed out with his right foot at the heavy table by his side.

'Ouch,' he added.

21

In Which our Hero Makes Some Interesting Discoveries

The following day I am sent on my rounds once more – the undertaker, the crematorium, the florist. On my return, Virginia silently steers me into the sitting room. She closes the door quickly and conspiratorially. I wonder if she will peek round the net curtains to check that nobody can over-hear us in the street, but she pulls me to the far side of the room, away from what I can only assume are her mother's ears.

'I've been talking to Mum,' she says.

This does not, on the face of it, appear to be a secret worth dragging me into the sitting room for.

'And?' I ask.

'I gave her the third degree to find out whether she knew Hugh was sending money to Malcolm and his family. I asked her if it could be blackmail.' She makes it sound as though this is fairly standard domestic conversation. Maybe it is from now on.

We had broken the news to her the previous evening of Malcolm's marriage, his death and his family's move to Horsham. She had received the news philosophically; though you could tell that she was disappointed that Malcolm would not be there to admire her new hat. Virginia had obviously taken discussions further in my absence.

'Did she know anything?' I say.

'She just looked puzzled and said he couldn't possibly have done. Paying my school fees was hard enough. There wouldn't have been anything left to send to Malcolm. And she couldn't understand why he would. She said she was sure Martin was wrong.'

'He could be,' I say. 'Don't forget that these overheard conversations took place years ago when he was six or seven – and he never dared discuss it with his mother after the first time.'

Virginia is silent, then says: 'It's funny, but it does sort of ring true. When I was younger, I always felt guilty about how much the school fees must be costing my parents. They would have been less then than they are now, but they were still quite hefty. Most of the girls at school lived in much grander houses than we did, and some were clearly pretty loaded. My father was a middle manager at a small company in London.'

'People make sacrifices . . .' I begin.

'But my parents didn't really,' she says. 'We never seemed short of cash – it's just that we didn't have a really big house or splash money around. I wondered sometimes if we were very rich but didn't want people to know. But that didn't seem too likely.'

I agree this was improbable. Rich people, in my experience, splash it about a bit. 'Do you know how much he left your mother?'

'She's being fairly cagey about that. I don't get the impression there are any problems. The solicitor is dealing with it.'

'If Malcolm had been blackmailing Hugh,' I say, 'do you think Hugh would have kept any letters from him or anything?'

'All gone, if he did,' says Virginia. 'He had apparently told my mother that, if anything happened to him (as they say), he wanted her to get rid of all his personal papers straight away. He didn't want them cluttering up the house for her, he said.'

'Very thoughtful. And so she . . .'

'Put them out for the recycling people, who collected them yesterday.'

I obviously do rush to the door just in case I can be fast enough to get there yesterday, but the green recycling box is empty except for a couple of take-away menus.

'There's nothing for it,' says Virginia. 'You are going to have to take my mother to one side, be frank with her, use all of your cunning, and get her to tell us exactly what happened.'

I carry out a quick inventory of my skills and assess my likelihood of success.

'Let's just get her drunk,' I suggest.

Virginia carries out a similar assessment of my competence. 'How much Bailey's is left?' she asks.

'There's an unopened bottle in the cupboard,' I say.

Virginia opens the door. 'Mum,' she calls invitingly, 'do you feel like a drink?'

* * *

It is late afternoon and I have got Daphne as drunk as I reasonably can. It is becoming clear that this was not a good plan. She is willing to tell us anything, but can no longer distinguish between truth and fantasy.

'Hugh was a *good* man,' she tells us for the tenth time. 'A good *man*. A good man. He was . . . who are we talking about?'

'Hugh,' I say.

'He was a good man,' she says.

Virginia is surprisingly not impressed. I am obliged to point out that it was a joint decision to get Daphne drunk. She points out that her first vote was that I did something useful for once. This is technically true, but . . .

I try again. 'Daphne, did Hugh never say why he sacked Malcolm?'

'He was a good man,' says Daphne.

'Hugh or Malcolm?'

'Yes,' says Daphne.

'Would anyone else know why he sacked him?'

'Hume,' says Daphne.

I mishear this as 'Hugh' the first time, which adds to the confusion, but she repeats the name.

'Hume?' I say.

'No,' says Daphne, 'just joking. Hume knows nothing.' She laughs.

I look at Virginia. She shrugs as if to say I've blown it and can't expect her to rescue me. I want to point out that this is her mother, not mine, but first I must focus on the job in hand.

'What doesn't Hume know?' I ask wearily. Daphne's eyes are closing slowly, and I'm not entirely sure Hume really exists other than in her imagination.

'Carbon paper,' says Daphne, as though she has suddenly woken up. She laughs. 'He really was a stupid man.' Then she adds, 'I'm not feeling very well. You'll have to excuse me,' and leaves the room quite quickly. It's a while before she returns, and by then she seems to have sobered up a little and to be more wary.

'Carbon paper?' I ask.

But Daphne looks at me blankly. 'What are you on about?' she asks. 'Nobody uses carbon paper these days.'

'Look, Mum,' says Virginia, 'why don't you have a little rest?'

Daphne agrees she might as well. Once she has gone, I assume I am in for an earful on the subject of ineffective detective work, but this is not what Virginia wishes to talk to me about. When her mother is clearly out of radar range she says: 'You realize we were onto something there?'

'We? I think I was asking the questions.'

'You may have asked the question, but you did not understand the answer.'

'Carbon paper?'

'No, I don't know what she meant by that either, but she realized she had let something slip and was rattled.'

'But, *carbon paper*?'

'Forget the stationery order. I've remembered who Hume was.'

'And?'

'He was one of the directors of the insurance company Hugh and Malcolm worked for.'

'That's hardly letting slip a major secret.'

'But he might know why Hugh sacked Malcolm. Mum pretty well told us he did.'

'If we can track him down,' I add. 'Once your mother's sober, she'll deny ever having heard of him.'

We turn immediately to Hugh's address book. A Colin Hume is listed.

'Hugh wrote this years ago,' I say. 'Look – that dialling code must have changed in the eighties.'

'But you can easily find the new code.'

'He may have moved. He could be dead. It figures that he was older than Hugh,' I point out.

'That's what you're going to find out,' says Virginia, thrusting the book into my hands. 'And there's no time like the present.'

'Why me?' I ask.

'It'll make him suspicious if I phone,' she says.

I have already finished dialling before I realize that this last remark is total crap. Then somebody answers the phone. 'Colin Hume speaking.' A two-minute conversation and we have fixed to see him later the same evening. That was easy.

No, actually, that was *too* easy. He wants to see us at least as much as we want to see him.

* * *

Another day, another semi – this time in Dorking.

Colin Hume proves to have the sort of piercing gaze that might worry you if you had anything to hide. In his middle age, which is to say some years ago, it must have been a very formidable gaze indeed. Even now, you wouldn't want to get in the way of it unless you had to, as we currently do. His hair is almost white and the thin strands look silky but tired. He retains a mild Scottish accent; my guess is he still supports the Scottish national rugby team but only so long as he can do it from an armchair in Dorking. He gives the impression of being quite happy and he probably is. If we have anything to offer him, it's not that much. The question is: does he have anything to offer us, and, if so, will he do it?

He sits us down, considerately moderates the intensity of the gaze for a bit, and pours us tea. This makes me very nervous. Over the past few days, nice hot drinks have usually been linked closely to shattering revelations. I try to cross my fingers as I pick up the plain white bone-china cup.

'I've been waiting for some years for this,' he says cheerfully, as if we have just offered to take him to the funfair. 'Mostly I thought I'd go to my grave not knowing the answer – and when you began by telling me Hugh was dead – my sincere condolences, by the way, Virginia – I was pretty certain that he'd taken the secret with him. But, then again, maybe not?'

'I don't know,' I say. 'We were hoping you'd tell us stuff rather than the other way round.' Still, I give him a bit of the story so far, while he just nods and occasionally reaches for one of the jammy dodgers, which are on a plate much closer to him than to us.

'I can tell you some things that you don't know,' he says. 'Back in the days when Hugh and Malcolm worked for me I was the director responsible for finance. All finance directors are a bit paranoid about fraud, but I was pretty certain I had one on my hands. It's like a bicycle tyre going flat – you may not know where the rusty nail has gone in, but you know fine you've got a puncture. We were overspending in all sorts of little ways, but it was when I looked at the stationery budget that I started to get worried. Insurance companies produced masses of paperwork in those days, so if you could skim off a few per cent it was worth the effort. These days I'd go for the IT budget. A few fake invoices for "software support" or operating-system licences aren't likely to be questioned outside the IT department itself. In those days it was . . . oh, just as an example . . . carbon paper or type-writer ribbons. If somebody queried the rising costs of non-existent orders you could just say: "Those useless girls in the typing pool – they use a sheet of carbon paper once and then throw it away. I'll have word with the supervisor," and then take credit for the saving and switch the swindle elsewhere. Anyway, for a few months I just monitored the stationery budget, and one or two others, very quietly. I was almost there when I stupidly took Hugh into my confidence to see if he knew anything. Then, young idiot that I was, I went off on leave, having asked him to do a bit of a snoop round. When I got back, he'd fired Malcolm. Hugh said he'd confronted him with it, Malcolm had admitted the fraud and Hugh had sacked him on the spot but "to protect the good name of the firm" had not reported it to the police. Malcolm had left quickly, present whereabouts unknown and unknowable. When I asked whether he'd had any accomplices, Hugh just looked blank and said that he hadn't really asked him. I was furious, but there was nothing to be done. In fact the losses did stop suddenly at that point, though that wasn't the end of the story. Later I picked up a number of cases where – how shall I put it? – we had unaccountably given our suppliers a better deal than they might have expected. I suspected somebody was taking a cut, but was never able to prove who it was. Hugh never seemed short of money – private school fees and all that – but he just said an aunt had died and left him a legacy. Do you know which aunt that might have been?'

Virginia shakes her head. 'I don't remember anyone leaving us anything, except the grandfather clock and a very old family Bible that my mother placed straight in the dustbin as being dirty and unhygienic.'

'Hmm. Well, I wouldn't want to call your father a liar . . .'

'Hugh wasn't my father.'

'All the same . . .'

'Hugh wasn't my father. If Malcolm knew something about Hugh it would explain how he could have been blackmailing him.'

'Was he?'

'Maybe,' says Virginia, biting her lip. 'I'd hoped to find letters from Malcolm, but they've all been recycled. Soon somebody will be opening a carton made from recycled paper and will wonder why the orange juice inside it tastes of wormwood and gall.'

'I always squeeze my own orange juice – most of the

carton stuff tastes a bit like that anyway. Still, even a hint of blackmail is promising. But I guess with Hugh and Malcolm both dead and me just a doddering old pensioner with an increasingly unreliable memory, we'll never know for sure. Even so, I'm 98 per cent sure that Hugh was ripping us off (as you young people say) and I'm 97 per cent sure that Malcolm was his loyal accomplice, even if Hugh did sacrifice him to save his own skin.'

'What,' I say, 'makes people commit fraud?'

Colin hesitates, as if he might be about to give away important information, then smiles and says: 'Opportunity.'

And that seems to be that.

Colin apologizes for the fact that he seems to have eaten all of the jammy dodgers and for the fact that they were the last he has. He does not seem very sorry. He declines Virginia's suggestion that he should attend the funeral on the grounds that there will just be a lot of old people there. He does not like the company of old people. 'But you two can come back and visit any time you wish,' he says brightly as we leave. 'My best wishes to your mother, Virginia. I always had a lot of time for her in the days when she worked for us.'

'Your mother seems to have had plenty of admirers,' I say to Virginia as we thread our way down the path, through the rose bushes.

'Runs in the family,' she says.

I raise an eyebrow.

'Only a joke,' she says. She kisses me on the cheek in reassurance and we return to the MG.

* * *

We are back in Hugh's study, staring at the empty shelves where Hugh's old correspondence may have been. All that is left are a few boxes, spared by Daphne, labelled with the names and numbers of regiments. I scan them quickly – '*The Buffs*', '*The Royal Welch Fusiliers*', '*The Suffolk Regiment*', '*KRRC*', '*150th Foot*', '*44th and 56th Foot*', '*A&S Highlanders*', '*Gurkhas*'. One or two relate to battles and battlefields. Lots of interesting stuff there all right, but not what we want.

That really is that then.

22

A Man of Letters

Or then again, maybe it isn't.

I awake (and therefore Virginia awakes) suddenly in the early hours of the morning. The room is dark. Only the illuminated dial of the bedside clock gives any clue as to precisely how ridiculous it is to be up and about. Nevertheless I am sitting up in bed and saying: 'There's no such regiment!' Virginia is replying: 'Why the hell did you wake me up at one o'clock in the morning for a lesson in military history?'

'There is,' I say, 'no 150th Foot, nor was there ever. So why did Hugh have a file on them?'

'How am I meant to know that? I'm going back to sleep. I'll deal with you in the morning, you moron.'

'Wait – where would you hide a tree?'

'Is this the arboreal Bishop Berkeley again? Because, if it is, you can tell him to sod off.'

'You would hide a tree in a forest,' I explain patiently.

'That would be really stupid. Trees are big. It would cost a fortune to transport a tree even a short distance. Anyway, who on earth would want to hide a tree?'

'Where would you hide a file of letters you didn't want anyone to read?'

'In a forest?'

'You're not really awake, are you?'

'I am just a bit awake, but that's just a bit more than I want to be. I'd like to be almost entirely asleep. In two minutes I shall be.'

'I bet there's something interesting in that box.'

'So do I, but it's nothing that is going to stop me going back to sleep.'

I am already out of bed and pulling on my (Hugh's old red tartan) dressing gown. Once in the study I quickly locate the red box file on the shelf and open it. By the time I have absorbed the first letter Virginia has crept in silently and is standing behind me, reading over my shoulder.

* * *

2 *May*

Dear Hugh,

This is to let you know where I am, as we agreed I would (see address above). It's just a B&B place until I can work out something more permanent. Let me add I've kept my side of the bargain and now I expect you to keep yours. A couple of thousand would be a good start. Enough said for the moment. Verb Sap, eh? Are you sure you always get to the post before Daphne does? I'd set up a PO Box so that you can collect mail from the post office if we are to continue this correspondence. Give Daphne my love anyway. She

has to know at least that I did not leave by choice.
I don't want her to think badly of me.

   Yours
   Malcolm

12 May

Hugh,

   Thanks for the cheque, but I did say a couple of
<u>*thousand*</u>*. It's all very well for you, sitting comfortably*
in Horsham with your family around you, but things
look very different alone in Hartlepool, I can tell you.
I've moved on to another B&B, so please note the
change of address. I'm not doing much, so I've had
plenty of time to think. I know we agreed to do things
the way we have because of Daphne and Virginia, and
I do want the best for both of them, but I can't help
wondering why either of us had to take the rap. You
could have told Hume that you'd looked into it all and
found nothing. Or you could have stitched up Jim or
Stan – Stan probably. Frankly, I thought we had
covered our tracks pretty well and . . . [subsequent
pages missing]

2 January

Hugh, you bastard, don't you dare keep throwing
Virginia at me. Yes, I do understand that bringing up a
child costs money and, yes, I do realize she is mine, but
Margaret and I have got a kid of our own on the way
now. We need <u>*more cash*</u>*. You must have a way of*
raising some – mortgage that expensive bloody house
of yours. I wish you had any idea how difficult it is to

get a proper job without references. We've moved again
as you will see – a bit of a rough area but a lot more
space for us when the baby arrives . . . [subsequent
pages missing]

[UNDATED DRAFT IN HUGH'S HANDWRITING]

~~*Malcolm, old boy*~~
~~*My dear Malcolm*~~
Dear Malcolm

~~*Your last letter frankly just made me cross.*~~ *I think*
you need to get a grip on yourself. I have dealt fairly
with you from beginning to end. There is little point
in trying to blackmail me and still less point in your
moving to Horsham. What good would that serve
~~*except to worry Daphne? And no, I haven't let her*~~
~~*know where you are. We agreed that your job was to*~~
~~*lie low and that mine was to make money. Well, you*~~
~~*can scarcely complain at the last cheque that I sent.*~~
~~*Bear in mind that there is little you can do to harm me*~~
~~*at this stage, but (trust me) I could destroy you just like*~~
~~*that.*~~ *You say you've finally got a job driving lorries.*
Well, that must be bringing in some cash? Just be
patient.

    Yours as ever
    Hugh

10 April

Dear Hugh,

    Thanks for the latest cheque. I do understand what
you say – that you are now taking all the risk and all I
have to do is pocket the bunce, but it is still not exactly

*what I would have chosen. Your suggestion that I
might assist your 'friends' and pick up a bit more
(or maybe a lot more) is obviously interesting, though
it would help to know a little about them. I suspect
the game you're playing now has rather higher stakes
than I would be comfortable with. Just make sure
you're not in deeper than you realize.*

*It worries me sometimes what would become of
Margaret and Martin if anything happened to me. We
get by, but there's not a lot to spare. I'm going to be in
Sussex shortly. Maybe we should meet up and you can
tell me a bit more about your Italian friends?*

Yours
Malcolm

19 May

Dear Hugh,

*Very firmly, NO. I agreed to do that one job for
you and that scared the life out of me. The money was
good, but, no, really, never again. I'm planning to stick
to lorry driving from now on – I'll just have to do a
few more shifts. It's legal and it's safe.*

*I hope you are continuing to destroy these letters
as agreed?*

Yours ever
Malcolm

[UNDATED DRAFT IN HUGH'S HANDWRITING]

Dear Margaret,

*Both Daphne and I were deeply saddened to hear
of Malcolm's death. It is a terrible thing for you and*

Martin. ~~I will do what I can for you, but you must understand (whatever Malcolm may have told you) that all debts were more than repaid a long time ago.~~ I simply cannot help you financially as you ask, much though I would like to. I certainly would not recommend moving to Horsham. House prices here are going through the roof, and Martin must be getting settled at his school where you are. I'll write again soon. In the meantime I regret that neither Daphne nor I will be able to attend the funeral.

    Deepest condolences
    Hugh

3 August

Dear Mr Dewey,

    This is just to let you know that we have completed on our purchase and will shortly be moving to Horsham. We'll virtually be neighbours. Won't that be fun? You fobbed poor Malcolm off with excuses, but you'll find me rather different. Malcolm left some papers that your employers and the police might find interesting. He must have spent hours at that photocopier the evening before he left. I doubt that you will want me dropping in to say hello to you and your lovely family, so could I suggest that we have tea one day at a discreet little cafe? You'll know Horsham better than I do, so I'll leave you to name the place and I'll let you know when you should be there.

    You won't find me unreasonable. You might have to take your daughter (or should I say my husband's love child?) away from that posh school of hers, but that

*will be a small sacrifice, I'm sure, in helping to ease
your guilty conscience.*

*Write to me at our new address. By the time you
read this we shall already be packing. Exciting, eh?*

Yours sincerely,
Margaret Biggenhalgh

10 September

Dear Mr Dewey,

*I assume you were responsible for that unpleasant
incident last night? Well, it takes more than that to
frighten me. You have only strengthened my determination to get what is mine and Martin's. I want to
see you again at the same place at 11.00 on Saturday.*

Margaret Biggenhalgh

14 September

Dear Mr Dewey,

*This is to let you know, as you will have guessed,
that I found our meeting entirely unsatisfactory. I am
willing to give you one last chance, but no more than
that, Mr Dewey. Then I think your employers might
be prepared to pay me for the information I have.*

Yours in deadly earnest,
M. J. Biggenhalgh

16 September

*All right. All right. You have proved your point.
Please just stop. I can't take any more of this. I'm not
frightened for myself but Martin was really upset this
morning, even though I kept him out of the sitting*

room until I could get it more or less straight again.
Let's try to resolve this without anyone getting hurt,
please. You at least owe me that.

If possible I should also like the framed pictures of
Malcolm returned to me. The silver frame is valuable
but that's not the point, obviously. I have very few
photos of any sort and Martin will certainly notice
that the pictures of his daddy have gone. Still, Malcolm
always said you were a bastard, so why am I surprised
at what you have got your people to do?

Usual place, usual time.

MJB

[undated]

I, Margaret Biggenhalgh, acknowledge that there is no
basis to the accusations that I have lately made against
Hugh Dewey regarding a fraud perpetrated entirely by
my late husband, Malcolm Biggenhalgh. I wish to make
it clear that these accusations were occasioned by spite
and malice. I undertake never to repeat them. I author-
ize Mr Hugh Dewey to make any use he wishes of this
statement, should I repeat these or similar falsehoods,
or should he feel that it is otherwise justified. I sign
this freely and willingly in an attempt to make amends.

Margaret Biggenhalgh

* * *

'Wow!' I say.

Virginia, though I can feel her presence behind me, says
nothing.

'It looks,' I say, 'as though he kept the early stuff for the addresses. That's why we have only the first page in each case. Still, the story is pretty clear. It fits in with what Martin was saying about break-ins when they first moved to Horsham. It would also seem to explain why they stopped suddenly, if Martin's mother basically caved in like that. I'm glad I never crossed Hugh. Fraud. Intimidation. Shady Italian friends. Not to mention lying to your mother (brave man) about Malcolm's whereabouts. I also doubt that he broke into houses himself. So I suspect that he did have "people" to do that sort of thing. In which case, I wonder what else he got them to do? He's beginning to come across as the Al Capone of Horsham. Malcolm was wise to get out while he could.'

From behind me there is a sudden sob, and I am once again comforting Virginia as best I can.

There you are. What was it I said about grief? It isn't one of these everyday things. One moment you think you're fine – the next, you're sobbing about something that happened twenty years ago, and which you thought you'd forgotten.

'When I was little, he was my daddy,' she eventually says with difficulty, and mainly to my shoulder. 'He did my shoes up, he read to me, he plaited my hair, he helped me with my homework, he taught me to play chess.'

'I know,' I say, because my father did all that sort of stuff too, other than plaiting my hair, which would have been a bit weird, even in the remote part of Denmark he came from.

'There's a sense of loss . . .' she begins, but she doesn't

end. It's a tricky sentence for her at the moment and even starting it is quite an achievement.

'I know,' I say. 'After all, I lost three members of my family.'

'Three?' she says, puzzled.

Then I remember I have never told her about Niels.

'Yes, three,' I begin.

23

Niels

Niels was my younger brother. He was brilliant, really brilliant. In all his time at our school there wasn't one occasion when he didn't get the best exam results in the whole year group. And he wasn't just a swot. He was always in the football team. He was always somewhere in the cricket team – usually opening the batting, because nobody else much wanted to. He set a record time in the school cross-country, which I think still hasn't been broken. And all of this without ever seeming to try that hard or to suggest that he thought any of it mattered. He was pretty quiet but had a few very good friends. He never got angry. If a fight with somebody looked likely, he just joked his way out of it.

He died before he had a proper girlfriend (though he had plenty of friends who were girls) but I am sure that he would have known all about commitment, without having to have it explained to him in simple terms. He would have left the loo seat down. He would have bought flowers on occasions when he did not need to apologize for anything at all. He would have thought the Sorensen-Birtwistle Revised was a bit childish, but would probably have been too polite to say so. He might have given me useful advice. Who knows? Had he lived, my life would have been utterly different.

But he died.

I think that I wasn't supposed to know, but somebody who was there let it slip that Niels was still breathing, still conscious, when they eventually got him out of the wreckage. I don't know how many hours after the crash it was, but he had been trapped in there, alive, with our dead parents. There was, I was told, no chance he could have lived, even if they had got to him faster. Pretty well every organ was damaged one way or another. Pretty well every bone was broken at least once. They said they had no idea how he could have hung on that long, or what sort of determination kept a body going when it was, really, just bloody mush and splintered bone. When we found that kitten in the road, Niels was the first thing that I thought of. Of course there was nobody to do for Niels what Hugh did for the kitten. They got him into the ambulance and attached all sorts of lines to him, because that was what they did rather than because there was any point in it. It was there, still at the crash scene, that he died. My own theory is that, so long as he was imprisoned in the dark, he clung to life. He didn't want to die like that. Once they got him out, and once he knew there was no hope, he chose to die there and then in the light of day. That's what I think anyway.

For a long time after that I would dream that I too was trapped in a metal case, unable to move, unable to see, scarcely able to breathe. It wasn't that Niels had been killed that gave me nightmares, but the long hours that he had spent waiting for death, clinging to the last thread of life, hoping they would find him in time to die where there were living people and you could see the sun.

Strangely I found an answer in philosophy. What if, I argued to myself, this was only my version of reality? Perhaps in another version, Niels's version, it was I who travelled up to the Lakes with our parents and Niels who, for some good reason, stayed at home and learned later of my death in the wreckage. And possibly I died quickly and painlessly. It need not then be the case that Niels suffered like that or at all. In another reality he could have become an actuary, married a nice girl and had a whole batch of children – called Mogens, Grethe, Lise and maybe dear little Christian, the messy baby of the family.

Of course, all that had implications for the rest of the world and the existence or not of everyone in my version of it. But, hey, I could handle that.

So I detached myself from reality for a bit and found that it wasn't so bad. There was nothing in my contract with the Foreign Office that demanded I should believe in the real world. When I left the Foreign Office and joined the Royal Society for Medical Education it was even less necessary.

There were plenty of advantages. If this was my own private reality, then I could well be immortal, for example. I might be able to will things to happen. And my outlook could justifiably be completely amoral. I didn't need anyone. I owed nothing to anyone.

Which is how we get to where we are today.

'I am so sorry,' says Virginia.

'It's not such a bad place to be,' I say.

'I never knew.'

'I never told you.'

'You should have done.' She reaches out and touches my hand. 'Why didn't you tell me?'

Another long pause.

'It's getting light,' I say, noticing the changing colour of the sky. Beyond the net curtains, beyond the thick leaded diamonds of window glass, the sky is grey, but promising soon to be flooded with red.

24

Hugh

We decide to question Daphne stone cold sober this time and ambush her as she comes down to make an early morning cup of tea. We show her the box. She reads everything thoughtfully, sipping the tea.

'Well, if I had to destroy that one too, he should have told me where it was,' she says, in a tone wives use only for discussing their husbands. 'Best not put it out for the recycling people though.'

'Did you know?' asks Virginia.

'I'd seen one of the Margaret Biggenhalgh letters before,' says Daphne, 'but I never mentioned it to anyone.'

'Yes, you did,' says Virginia. 'You told me that you had found a letter from a Woman.'

'So I did,' says Daphne, conversationally. 'I'd forgotten that. It was in the kitchen. We were drying up. It wasn't any of the letters you have there, though – that one was quite friendly, really. Hugh must have thrown it away or hidden it somewhere else. Of course, one letter on its own didn't mean very much.'

'And the money?' asked Virginia. 'You must have noticed there was more money around than there should be.'

'I realized that there must be money coming in from somewhere.' Daphne sighs. 'There were people that your father – Hugh – used to meet. I don't think they were necessarily very nice people. He thought that I didn't know where he went, but I did.'

'You mean you followed him?' asks Virginia.

'Not every time. Then there were the business trips to Naples. Obviously I couldn't just get on the bus and follow him there, but even I realized that a small British insurance company would not be doing that much legitimate business in southern Italy.'

'Wait a minute,' I say. 'Are you implying Hugh was a member of the Mafia?'

'Oh, I doubt that it was anything as grand as that. Hugh didn't like joining things unless they were connected with military history. He never joined the Rotary Club, for example. I don't think he would have joined the Mafia either. But I think he knew people who were members of the Mafia or something very much like it. Your father – Hugh – did not take me much into his confidence, but I did work out most of it. It was helpful that Hugh always assumed I was stupid. You can learn quite a lot that way. He never told me anything about Malcolm though.'

'Don't you feel just a little bit betrayed?' asks Virginia.

'No more than usual,' says Daphne. 'He did it for you, Virginia. He only wanted to give you the very best. He would have died for you.'

'And would he have killed for me?'

'What a silly question,' says Daphne. 'Both of us would have killed for you if we'd had to. That goes without saying.'

* * *

It's the last leg of a long journey. I am driving Virginia back to London and to her flat in Clerkenwell. The journey is mainly undertaken in silence. We both have a lot to be silent about.

'I'd still like to say a few words at the funeral,' I venture as we reach the South Bank. 'Hugh may have been a Mafioso, but my hunch is that he was a nice Mafioso. The sort of Mafioso you'd really want to buy your car insurance from.'

'Do you think guys in shiny suits and very dark sunglasses will show up at the crematorium?' asks Virginia. 'It may not only be colleagues from the insurance world who've heard that he's died.'

'I'll watch out for them,' I say. 'If I see some, I'll cut some of the Mafia jokes from the speech.'

'My mother could have been making it all up or just plain wrong. Mothers *are* wrong more often than not, in my experience. I don't remember Dad . . . Hugh . . . making trips to Italy more than once or twice. That would make him a pretty half-hearted Mafioso, wouldn't it?'

'So where did the school fees come from?'

'They were cheaper then.'

'Hugh must have been a bit of a crook though.'

'Yes, but only a bit. I'll tell the undertakers we won't need the full gangland funeral.'

'That's a shame,' I say. 'I've always wanted to go to a proper gangland funeral.'

Obviously, I have no way of knowing that I won't be going to Hugh's funeral. That knowledge comes later, though not very much later.

I drop Virginia off in Rosebery Avenue. We agree that the next time we meet will probably be in Horsham. I kiss her on the cheek and she skips lightly up the steps, her skirt swaying from side to side, and vanishes into the block of flats. I still haven't asked her to marry me, but there's plenty of time for that. My immediate concerns are slightly different.

For some time now I have successfully avoided thinking about the reception I will receive tomorrow at work, when Humph will fill me in on recent developments in the Digby Spain saga and let me know whether I still have a job. Or not. What I need to do urgently, therefore, is to phone Fat Dave and get him to buy me a drink. After all, it's his round.

25

Stockholm, January 1650

It was cold. So very cold.

The giant, iron-bound rear wheels of the ornate royal coach crunched through the snow in the wake of the two smaller front wheels and the sixteen clattering iron-shod hooves. The previous day, the sun had melted the surface a little, but the merciless chill of a clear, starry night had frozen everything even harder than before. It was one of the coldest winters in memory, during a century that would not be noted for its warmth. And this was the coldest time of day, if day could be said to exist at all in January in Sweden. It would be another five hours until the sun rose. Then much the same before it set again. It was a good place to own a candle shop.

The philosopher, though huddled in several layers of fur, shivered. He pulled the softest of the pelts up as far as his grey, but carefully trimmed beard. This was an hour to be in bed, preferably in the company of a pretty and compliant member of the opposite sex, not a time to be bouncing over hard and rutted black ice in a coach with primitive suspension and a coachman instructed to get you to your destination in good time rather than in good condition. He could try telling the coachman to slow down, but he knew it would make no difference. Somebody who can get the greatest philosopher of the seventeenth century out of bed at half past four on a winter morning was not going to take any lip from a mere coachman if he dared to arrive a couple of minutes late. And in any case, if it was cold down here amongst the sables and reindeer skins, it must be quite a lot fresher up on the coachman's box, with nothing except the royal livery between you and the clear night sky. The coachman had more than one reason for wanting to get this journey over as quickly as he could.

'Ooof,' observed the philosopher as they hit a particularly resistant rut.

The philosopher listened out for the church bells, as probably did the coachman. The bells had rung the half-hour from their several dark, granite towers some time ago. The moment they rang the new hour in, she would be pacing up and down in her chamber, increasingly impatient and increasingly petulant. You keep queens waiting at your peril.

The philosopher banged on the roof of the carriage with his stick and yelled: '*Plus vite! Hurtig! Allez!*'

This request was answered immediately with the crack of a whip, and the philosopher was flung backwards into his seat. As the works of a number of clocks ticked unstoppably towards announcing the new hour, a coach containing an elderly French philosopher lurched on recklessly through the pitch-black, narrow and closely shuttered streets of old Stockholm.

* * *

You had to admit it. She looked magnificent in that ermine dressing gown (or whatever it was) seated by the regally vast and dangerously spitting fire of birch and pine logs. Hardly more than a girl really, but well used to exercising power and perfectly aware of the effect she had on men, hence not doing the dressing gown right up to her throat, or even close to her throat really. Could she be wearing anything at all underneath it? Best not to speculate, especially if you were an elderly French philosopher in unavoidable exile. The palace was full of courtiers (and one rather elderly philosopher) wishing they were thirty years younger.

Few courtiers got what the philosopher got, however: five hours of the Queen's uninterrupted and uninterruptible attention, three times a week, even if those hours were from five to ten in what the Swedes deluded themselves was 'morning'. Fortunately the candle shops kept the palace well supplied.

The subject of today's tutorial was the soul, the body and the union between the two, which the philosopher thought might be a more promising topic than optics or mathematics. But the Queen's attention was already starting to drift.

'Do you think I should invade Portugal?' she asked.

'Portugal?' asked the philosopher.

'Portugal.'

'It is a long way away, Your Majesty.'

'It is close to Spain. I am contemplating an alliance with the King of Spain.'

'In what way has Portugal offended you?'

'Portugal is the enemy of my future ally. We shall invade the silly little country, two kings together.'

And that was another of the Queen's small peculiarities – she thought she was a king. Easy to let that one slip your memory, but fortunately the mode of address was identical.

'Your Majesty,' said the philosopher, 'I thought that perhaps this morning – to the extent that this can be described as morning we might look at the soul, the body and the—'

'Don't philosophers have anything to say about love?' the Queen demanded.

'Love, Your Majesty?' Where was this leading?

'That's right: love.'

'The Greek philosophers did, Your Majesty, but it was often about love between men and men rather than between men and women.'

The Queen pulled a face. 'Meaning . . . ?'

'They didn't go into detail,' said the philosopher.

'Have you ever been physically attracted to another man, Monsieur Descartes?'

Descartes considered. He was at an age when he felt he should be able to answer such a question honestly. Had he? There was usually something behind all of the Queen's questions. Maybe best to stay silent then.

The Queen (briefly forgetting she was a king) stroked the fur of her robe for a moment, running her hand slowly down from her shoulder to her thigh. It suddenly occurred to the philosopher that she must be very lonely. 'Philosophers must fall in love sometimes, Monsieur Descartes,' she said.

'Yes,' said Descartes. 'As often as other people, I would imagine.'

'But you never married? Never had children?'

'I never married,' said Descartes. 'But I did have children. Well, one child anyway.'

'Did have?'

'She died. She was quite young.'

'What was her name?'

For a moment Descartes was unable to say anything, but eventually he got a single word out. 'Francine,' he said.

'It's a lovely name.'

Descartes sniffed, nodded and looked at the fire, which was just starting to warm him.

'And her mother? Is she still alive?'

'Possibly,' said Descartes, turning back to the Queen. 'I've really no idea.'

'I have been meaning to ask you something,' said the Queen suddenly.

'That's what I'm here for,' said Descartes.

'Do you think I should become a Catholic?'

There were, of course, two answers to this: yes and no. Both seemed fraught with danger – for the Queen and (more immediately) for the person advising her.

'That is not something that is within my remit,' said Descartes, who had heard rumours and was not entirely unprepared.

'I thought that, as a Jesuit, you would welcome the opportunity to convert me.'

'I was trained by Jesuits, Your Majesty,' said Descartes. 'I am not a Jesuit myself. Just a Catholic.'

'So, you must believe that Catholicism is right and that all Protestants will go to hell?'

That, of course, was the problem. Should he be complicit in sending the Queen of Sweden to hell simply in order to retain a relatively comfortable post in his old age? Surely a low probability of eternal damnation was an acceptable risk?

'I have,' said Descartes thoughtfully, 'lived a long time amongst Protestants and they have treated me more kindly than the Catholic church would have done – if it could have got its hands on me, which is something I have worked hard to avoid. Protestants have certainly proved more friendly to philosophy of late than my own Church has and Protestant rulers – such as you are – have offered me more protection than Catholic rulers. My personal view is that . . . not *all* Protestants will go to hell, though I rather hope Professor Voetius of Utrecht does. In more practical terms, a Catholic queen . . . or indeed king . . . would never be allowed to rule Lutheran Sweden, which would be a bit inconvenient for you.'

'I could abdicate.'

'It must be very lonely to be a monarch,' said Descartes after a long pause.

'That isn't the point,' said the monarch.

'The immediate and pressing point, Your Majesty,' said Descartes, glancing nervously over his shoulder, 'is that this type of talk is dangerous. I accepted your invitation to come here in part – though obviously not entirely – because it was safer than France or even Holland. I haven't declined being burnt as a heretic in order to be sent to the block for trying to subvert the ruler of Sweden. I hope, Your Majesty, that you haven't discussed this with anyone else? Or if you have, I hope that you have not mentioned my name?'

The Queen said nothing to reassure him and then asked: 'And how is the French Ambassador?'

'Monsieur Chanut is making a good recovery at last. Pneumonia need not prove fatal, given proper care.'

The Queen sighed. 'It is our harsh northern climate. You must keep warm at all costs, Monsieur Descartes. I am unreasonable in expecting you to attend upon me so early and in this cruel weather. You *must* tell me when I am being unreasonable.'

Descartes shrugged, but in a hopeful way. Should he suggest a ten o'clock start? Or maybe even eleven?

'I shall instruct them to put more furs in your coach,' said the Queen decisively.

'I am very grateful to Your Majesty for your concern,' said Descartes, who had always known deep down that queens, and indeed kings, conceded very little, and this one (whichever she was) less than most. 'Would you like me to continue with the lesson?'

'Of course,' said the Queen brightly. 'That's what you're here for, isn't it?'

26

London

I am halfway through my first pint before Dave finally shows his face. I hate it when people keep you waiting.

'My round,' he says, without prompting. 'Same again? Pint of Shires?'

'Shires is a fictitious brewery, whose products are available only in the equally fictitious village of Ambridge,' I point out.

'All tastes the same to me,' says Dave. 'I'll just get whatever bitter they serve here.'

He bustles off to the bar and returns with two foaming pint glasses. Even so I'm thinking: All tastes the same to me? This is not the way Dave normally talks.

'What do you mean – it all tastes the same?' I enquire politely. 'Have you suddenly turned into some sort of effete, Babycham-drinking Spurs supporter, Birtwistle?'

He shrugs. 'How's Virginia? It must be tough on her with her father suddenly dying like that. Tough on you too. How old was he?'

'Early sixties.'

'No age,' says Dave with a shake of the head.

'I thought you reckoned anyone over fifty must be senile,' I say.

'No, just you,' says Dave.

'I'm not over fifty,' I say.

Dave gives a grin and takes a long pull on the pint glass. He wipes the back of his hand across his mouth in his usual slobbish manner. Some things are still reassuringly the same then.

'What was the trip north all about?' he asks.

I give him a quick résumé of the past few days, omitting items such as my sobbing on Virginia's shoulder and Hugh's links with the Mafia, but playing up my role in the pursuit of Malcolm through Grasmere and excellent detective work generally.

He nods appreciatively. 'And how are things between you and Virginia now?'

'Good,' I say. 'I think we might just be about to get married.'

'Congratulations,' he says, without any hint of irony. 'How's Lucy going to take that?'

'I'm sure she'll be very brave,' I say.

'Dumped you, did she?'

'Not in so many words.'

'Whatever,' he says. 'Still, well done. I'm really pleased for both of you. You and Virginia, that is; though Lucy seems to have made a sound choice too.' He looks for a moment as though he is about to shake my hand in a vigorous and manly fashion, but I offer no encouragement.

'And how has your week been?' I ask slightly patronizingly, as you do when you've had the sort of time I've had.

'Quite eventful too,' he says.

There is one of those deliberate pauses. I'm supposed to ask what has happened, but I have a feeling of foreboding.

'Well, since you ask so eagerly,' he continues, 'I'm getting married to Megan.'

'Married to Megan?'

'If Virginia will put up with you, why not Megan and me?'

'Good point,' I concede, though frankly I see no comparison of any sort. 'So are you going to let me have a date so I can get working on my best man speech? I've got a few anecdotes I've been saving up for just such an occasion. I might just tell the one about you in the bar in Corfu . . .'

I stop because I am not getting any of the reactions I expect. 'OK, not the Corfu story then,' I say. 'What? Why are you looking at me like that?'

'I've asked Pete to be best man,' he says.

'Pete?'

'My brother Pete.'

'I know who Pete is,' I say. 'That clearly isn't what I meant.'

'Sorry.'

'It's your funeral,' I say.

'Wedding,' he says.

'Same thing.'

We both drink for a bit, then he says: 'Sorry.'

'Don't keep saying it,' I say. 'It's fine. It's all fine. We're still mates.'

Actually, it is fine, but Dave feels the need still to explain and make it even better than that. This is usually a bad plan.

'It's just . . .' he begins. 'It's just that Megan doesn't see you as a very good influence on me.'

'*Me*? On *you*?' You'll have to agree it seems a bit rich. But didn't somebody else say the same thing to me recently?

'She says I'm quite normal when I'm with her, but that when I'm with you we seem to be trying to outdo each other in coarseness and male chauvinism. Don't blame me: it's just that's what she says.'

This too seems to be something I have heard before. It's untrue; I'm simply conceding I might have heard it before.

'Well, obviously,' I say. 'It's what us lads do.'

'Not at your age,' he says.

I say nothing.

'How old are you, Chris?'

I say nothing.

'Forty-three?'

I say nothing.

'You and Pete were already in the sixth form when I was in the first form, and I'm thirty-six. So you're forty-three? Forty-four?'

'Forty-two,' I say indignantly. 'I'm hardly out of my thirties. Call it thirty-twelve.'

'Good old Chris,' he says.

'Meaning what?' I say.

'Never face up to reality unless you have to.'

'And your point is?'

'Nothing.'

'Don't worry,' I say, 'I'll come to the wedding even if I'm not best man.'

There is another pause.

'You *are* inviting me to the wedding?' I say.

'I'm sure she'll come round to it,' he says.

'She doesn't even want me at the wedding? How often has she even met me? Once? Twice?'

'Often enough,' he says with an awkward smile. He'd like to make a joke of it, but I'm not going to let him.

'I can't believe I'm hearing this,' I say. 'This isn't happening.'

'Good old Chris,' he says uncertainly.

'Well, you'll be best man at my wedding anyway . . .' Then I see from Dave's expression that this too is not a foregone conclusion.

'One day at a time, eh?' he says.

'Dave, we're supposed to be *mates*.'

'We'll always be mates,' he says. I just wish he sounded a bit more convinced.

'Mates invite each other to their weddings,' I point out.

'Oh, for God's sake,' he says with a sudden fierceness that I don't remember seeing before. 'Does it *really* matter? I had Megan on about it all last night. It looks as if I'll have you on about it all tonight. Fine, have it your own way – we're not mates. At least I won't have to sit here and listen to your inane middle-aged ramblings all evening. At least I won't have to listen to you trying to pretend to be twenty-five again. At least I won't have to hear the stories about you chatting up girls half your age. At least I won't have to buy your bloody beer for you all the time. If we're not mates then that is perfectly in order.'

'So that's how you see me? A pathetic, balding, middle-aged bloke trying to be twenty and leching after teenage girls.'

'You missed the bit about not buying your rounds.'

I ignore this slur and repeat the teenage girls stuff.

'I said half your age – that wouldn't make them teenagers by a couple of years,' he says with a forced grin. He goes to punch me on the arm, but I pull back. He shrugs. 'Oh, come on. I didn't mean it. It's just that Megan has been giving me grief about the guest list generally – not just about you. Too many of my friends, she says, and not enough of her family. Not enough of either set of friends, I say, and too many relations generally. It's all a bit tense at the moment. I'll sort it out. You'll be at my wedding and Megan and I will be at yours. We're mates, OK?'

'But that *is* how you see me? That *is* how you've always perceived me?'

'What does it matter how I perceive you?'

'*Esse est percipi*,' I observe.

'Meaning?'

'Meaning, if people see you as a pathetic fraud, then you are a pathetic fraud.'

'OK, fine. You're a pathetic fraud. You said it. Not me. But I'll agree with you, if that's what floats your boat. OK? Look, Chris, I don't mind the crap jokes, but just spare me the self-pity. You're old enough to know better.'

I realize that all I need to do is to say sorry for over-reacting, to agree that it doesn't matter if I go to the wedding or not, to offer to buy a round. In due course a gold-edged invitation will come my way. We'll go and watch Southend lose to Colchester at Roots Hall. This need not be the end of a beautiful friendship.

'Go to hell,' I therefore suggest to him. 'And take your stupid football team with you.'

'Arsenal or Southend?' He seems genuinely curious.

'Stuff them both.'

'Whatever,' he says. He won't even argue with me now.

But you can always find a new angle on a quarrel if you try hard enough.

'So,' I say, jabbing my finger at him, 'I'm just this sad old bastard who makes crap jokes and . . . and . . .' I'm not sure I do want to run though the entire list of my faults, even if I could put it together. Still, you have to admit, it's a start. Sad bastard. Crap jokes. Old.

'It would be a shame if we all aged gracefully,' he says. 'Come on, Chris, let's have another beer. My round.'

'I never asked to be forty-two,' I say.

'Nobody does.'

'How would you know?'

'Chris, who cares? Who gives a monkey's? Do you want another sodding beer or not?'

'No.'

'Then go and sulk somewhere else.'

'As you wish, David.' I stand up.

'Sorry, I didn't mean that either.' He shakes his head and looks down at the table.

I turn sharply on my heel and stride in the direction of the door. I open it and let it swing behind me as I step into the street. I do not look back.

27

A Bad Day at Work

Another Monday. Can't believe it's only a week since the last one.

As I leave the train at Great Portland Street I spot Narinder just ahead of me. I slow my pace just enough to allow a few people to pass me and act as a shield, then follow on, keeping my head well down. I still have a lot of thinking to do before I get to the office – for example, the precise wording of my resignation letter.

The brave thing, of course, would be to go straight to Humph's office and own up. I am therefore just sneaking past his door when I hear him call my name. I stop and wait for the inevitable dressing down.

'Welcome back,' he says. 'Good to see you, Chris. I trust you've managed to sort things out?'

I look at him, puzzled.

'You said in your email that you had personal matters to sort out,' he says.

'Yes,' I say cautiously. 'All sorted.'

'Well, I'm sure you'll be busy on your first day back. I'll catch you later.'

I am still standing there. This is not going according to plan. Hasn't he forgotten to sack me?

He seems to realize that I am waiting for something else because he quickly adds: 'Oh yes, sorry – well done on the George Magwitch story.'

There does not seem to be a note of heavy irony in his voice.

'The story?' I say.

'Didn't you see Digby Spain's article?'

'I haven't looked at a paper for days.'

'Then take a look at this,' he says, passing me a well-thumbed press cutting. 'I'm thinking of having it framed.'

I glance at the headline. '**Former Care Worker Exposed as Benefit Cheat**,' it reads.

'Very clever of you to feed that to Digby Spain,' says Humph. 'Once he'd run the piece and the authorities had decided there would have to be charges, Dan Smith's other claims started to look a bit silly. There's no real connection between the two things, of course, but there are plenty of people out there would think that if you can lie to the benefits agency then you probably beat up old people as well. It's all a matter of perception. You are what people think you are. Now everyone's giving him a good kicking.'

'Where one dog pisses, many dogs shall piss,' I say.

'Sorry?' says Humph.

'Just a saying.'

'Is it? If you say so, Chris. Anyway, Barbara Proudie's stuck by him. You have to admire her determination, I suppose. Most of Dan Smith's other supporters have jumped ship though, including that MP. I saw Smith on television last night – doesn't know what's hit him, poor man. He should never have agreed to be interviewed, but he's got nobody left to advise him on that sort of thing, I guess. Obviously his case against George Magwitch is exactly the same as it was before, but the bottom line is that Smith's lost the will to pursue it. He certainly doesn't have the stomach to take it to the GMC. You could call that a result.'

'Thanks for letting me know,' I say.

'Take the cutting away and read it.'

I shake my head. 'I've got the general drift,' I say.

'Well done, anyway,' says Humph. 'That was excellent work. It showed good judgement. One other thing, though . . .'

'Yes?'

'Why did you tell everyone I was dying?'

'I thought you said . . .' I begin. But I can't remember what it was that he did say. 'I thought you were looking a bit . . . tired.'

'Tired?'

'A bit.'

'And – let me get this straight – my looking a bit tired caused you to make a general announcement that I had weeks to live?'

Actually it was only Jon that I told, but that maybe isn't the point, so I say: 'You're OK then?'

'Fine. Just a bit tired, as you so rightly deduced.'

'That's good,' I say, trying to stress the positives, though I still need a bit more explanation.

'It was my wife, Mary, who was ill. She's a lot better now,

but it was tricky for a while, getting her to and from hospital and then trying to be here at nine, making up the time whenever I could.'

'But you said you were leaving . . .'

'Mary's been pretty sick. At times like that you realize that you may not have as many years of good health as you'd hoped. So I'm retiring a year or two early. We're going to spend a year travelling, then I might look for something part-time, but I've had enough of this place. That's all. Nothing sinister.'

'I'm sorry – but it was only Jon that I mentioned it to.'

'You couldn't expect him not to be concerned. He told Brindley and Brindley told . . . well, let's just say it got around.'

'Right,' I say.

'No harm done, but if you're not sure about something, then check. I think they were collecting for a wreath by the time I found out what was going on.'

As I enter my own little kingdom, Jon and Narinder both stand and applaud.

'Welcome back,' says Jon. 'Well done on the Magwitch story. You should have let me in on it, but I forgive you.'

'Welcome back,' says Narinder.

Fatima, looking slightly puzzled as usual, stays seated and flashes me a quick smile. Lucy's desk is empty. Doubtless somebody will fill me in on that one, but for the moment it's fine by me.

This is the appropriate moment for the quick one-liner,

and there is an expectant pause, but I just say: 'It's good to be back. I'll check my emails and catch up with you later.'

Before I can switch the PC on, however, the phone rings.

'Hello, Chris,' says George Magwitch. 'Am I catching you at a bad time?'

'It's fine,' I say.

'Well, Digby came up trumps in the end, eh? Where did you find out about the benefit fraud by the way?'

'You told me.'

'Did I? I don't think so. Digby says you gave him the dirt. He checked it out like the good and thorough journalist that he is. Actually, he asked Smith a few not-too-searching questions and Dan Smith, not being the sharpest knife in the box, gave him decent, honest answers. And the rest, as they say, is history. Well done. Of course, the fact that Digby and I were at school together may also have helped.'

'Were you?'

'Well, not at the same time – he's a bit younger than I am. That's why I didn't recognize the name when you first put us in touch. But, chatting to him the second time round, it turned out we had both been to the same place – same house, actually. Always useful, eh? Didn't I mention it in my email?'

'No.'

'Maybe not. I'm always pretty careful what I put in emails. You never know whose hands they'll fall into, don't you think?'

'Very true.'

'Anyway, Chris, I'm sure you must be busy, but I just wanted to say thank you for all your help.'

'My pleasure,' I say.

When I put the phone down, Jon looks round the door. 'Was that Barbara Proudie?' he asks.

'No,' I say.

'Thank goodness for that,' he says. 'I forgot to warn you she's been phoning almost hourly. She is well hacked off. I've been fielding her calls while you were away. Where *were* you anyway?'

'It's a long story,' I say.

'Why didn't you phone me or reply to any of my emails? There was one point where we were going crazy. Roger had heard a rumour that Digby Spain was going to dissect Magwitch. It was only when we saw the article that we realized you'd been a lot smarter than we thought. Even so, next time, tell me what you're up to if you're going to talk to the press. And at least keep your mobile switched on when you're away, unless you'd like me to have a nervous breakdown.'

'I'll try to remember,' I say. Then I pluck up courage and add: 'Where's Lucy?'

'Sorry – I would have told you that too if you'd phoned me last week. She quit.'

'Because of me?'

'Don't flatter yourself. She just got an offer of more money elsewhere. One day she was here, the next she'd gone. No apology. No notice. Kids these days, eh?'

'Yeah,' I say. 'Kids these days.'

In the office outside a phone rings. Fatima calls to me: 'It's Barbara Proudie. Should I put her through?'

I take the call. As usual, I am not required to say much.

'Well, Christian, I suppose you're all feeling pretty pleased with yourselves?'

'Not especially,' I say.

'You have completely destroyed Dan Smith, you know that? Digby Spain tricked him into admitting that he had claimed some tiny sum of money that he wasn't entitled to – just because it made a good story. Just for the story, Christian. Do you know, Christian, what it's like to be poor – to be really poor? The care home hardly paid him a fortune, but it was work. Once they'd sacked him, nobody else was going to take him on. Do you know what it's like to apply for job after job and not even get an interview? Dan Smith had a pregnant wife and three children to support – on benefits he was perfectly entitled to, Christian. Then somebody told him it would be OK if he worked a couple of days a week stocking shelves at the supermarket and that he did not need to declare it to the benefits people. A bloke in a pub told him. People like Dan can't afford to consult lawyers and don't trust officials of any sort. Officials don't trust them either. They don't have the money to buy computers and check it out on the Internet. So, he took the advice of the bloke in the pub, and December was the one time when it was easy to get a part-time job – even for him. So he worked nights to try to get enough money to buy the children Christmas presents. Not flashy new bikes or computer game things, Christian, just something so that when the kiddies went back to school after Christmas they wouldn't have to say to the other children that their family was too poor to buy them anything at all. And he didn't tell anybody he was working because the bloke in the pub said it was OK not to. Do you know what it's like to have no money?'

'No,' I reply, without really thinking too much about

what I'm saying. 'I've always been very well off, really. Since my parents died anyway – they left me the house and stuff, you see. Financially, at least, I've been fine.'

Barbara chooses not to pick up on this last remark. She's not a great listener anyway. But she can talk. 'You're all the same. It's like the investigators who tricked him into saying that his parents had always given him a good hiding when he was naughty and that was the best way to deal with things.'

'But that *is* what he thought?'

'He's a good man, just not too bright. He had no training, no supervision to speak of at that place. He just did as he was told.'

'So, basically, guilty as charged,' I say.

'No,' says Barbara. 'In fact, I think he was the only one at the care home not abusing the inmates. He didn't want to tell tales on his colleagues though, and ended up taking the blame.'

'Sounds like misplaced loyalty to me.'

'He's spent most of his life out of work. They gave him a job. They made him feel wanted.'

'But he knew what was going on. He should have reported it.'

Barbara for once says nothing.

'Look, he's been cleared of the charges of assaulting people at the home,' I say, 'when as far as I can see he was at least an accessory. He's been unlucky to be caught claiming benefits he wasn't entitled to. But, in the end and when you balance it all up, there's a sort of natural justice to the final result.'

'Natural justice?' she says wearily. 'Do you seriously call this outcome just? His life is ruined, Christian. The punishment for being a bit stupid, and for standing by work-mates he trusted and liked, is that in all likelihood nobody will ever employ him again, nobody will ever respect him again. Do you have any idea what that will be like?'

'I don't know,' I say. But she's right. I know nothing about people like Dan Smith. They occupy a different reality.

'I'm sure you don't,' she says. 'I just hope you are proud of what you've done. Are you, Christian? Are you?'

The line goes dead before I can decide whether I am or not. This must be the shortest conversation I've ever had with her. I slump back in my chair and breathe a sigh of relief. Finally I get to press the button at the front of my computer and watch it boot up. I go first to my emails. There are over three hundred (307) unread messages. I wonder where to start, then I notice something is wrong. There is something about the screen in front of me that is different. It takes a few seconds to realize it is because there is nothing (0) in the DRAFTS folder. So I must have deleted the dumping email to Virginia. Or conversely . . .

I click on SENT.

Dear Virginia,

I doubt that this email will come as a surprise to you. You must have noticed how we have been growing apart lately. It's not your fault. You need somebody more mature than I am. You need somebody who is ready to make a lifetime commitment. I on the other hand am not sure what I want or need. I am not Mr Right. I am not even Mr OK. One of the few things Dave has said that you'll agree with (eventually) is that you deserve better than me. I am offering

you the chance to find that person. Virginia, you are a
wonderful woman who will one day make some lucky man
a wonderful wife. I hope you can forgive me and that we
can remain friends.

With much affection, Chris

Yes, that seems pretty much as I remember it and, on reflection, clear enough for anyone. Excellent drafting, Chris. The
question is: has she seen it yet? I know she didn't check her
emails while we were away. There is that option that allows
you to recall an email that you've sent, but the first thing
I always do when somebody tries to recall one is to go and
read it simply to see what they were so embarrassed about –
it's usually quite rewarding. Maybe if I phone her quickly I
can get her to delete it unread. I'll say it was something Fat
Dave put me up to when we were both pissed. She'll believe
that. I just need to act fast.

* * *

The phone seems to ring for ever before Virginia answers.

'Hi,' I say.

'Hi,' she says, but her voice is a little odd.

'You opened the email,' I say.

'That's what you do with them,' she says. 'Somebody
sends you an email. You open it. You read it. I actually read
yours first. I thought it would be something nice.'

'Delete it and forget I sent it.'

'But you did.'

'Not intentionally.'

'So you never planned to dump me by email?'

'It was a joke,' I say feebly and improbably.

'That's worse,' she says.

'Is it?'

'Well, maybe marginally better,' she concedes. 'But . . .'

I remember that I was going to blame Dave. Still worth trying? Probably not.

'Hang on,' I say. 'We can't do this over the phone. We need to meet. We need to talk. There's a Starbuck's round the corner.'

'No, let's meet at the Costa in Marylebone High Street.'

'OK, see you there.'

'See you there, Puppy.'

As I hang up a thought crosses my mind: that's the last time she'll ever call me Puppy. But, no, there's still got to be hope.

As I sprint for the pedestrian crossing at the Euston Road I think: If the sign stays green until I am across then Everything Will be All Right. The lights are still green as I spring from the pavement and I watch them, my heart in my mouth, until my foot hits the central reservation.

Green!

Virginia is already there at a table, her coffee untouched in front of her. She looks up as I come in and gives me a half-smile. But her eyes are those of a stranger. A stranger that I'm never going to get to know.

'Don't you want to get a coffee?' she asks, just a little too politely, as I sit down.

'I didn't mean it,' I say, cutting to the chase. 'You have to believe that.'

(Silence.)

'OK, maybe I did mean it then, but I don't now. I've changed,' I add.

This is true. I don't know when I fell in love with her; all I know is that I did. Love, grief – it's like I say, you can't predict it.

'I know you've changed,' says Virginia slowly. 'The problem is: so have I.'

'I don't see the problem.'

'No change in that respect, at least.'

'Explain it for me.'

'Do I really need to? All right. You may not have meant to send it, but everything you said in it was true. I know it and you know it. We *have* been growing apart. I did need somebody who wanted to make a commitment.'

'I'll make a commitment if that's what I have to do.'

'*Wanted* to, Chris. Not *had* to. There's a whole world of difference in that one word. I understand you heaps better after the trip. My heart really goes out to you. I understand why . . . you have problems with relationships. I can see what has happened to you would make you sort of detached. I can see why commitment might be a problem. But that's why I have to let you go. I'm the wrong person for you.'

'I've changed,' I say again.

She nods.

'Look,' I say, 'before we went to Grasmere, I really did think the relationship was at an end. But when we were there

– sorry: this sounds a bit corny – I really, genuinely fell in love with you. It's OK. I love you, Virginia.'

'But you were planning to dump me,' she points out, not unreasonably.

'Well . . . OK . . . yes, *then* possibly, but not *now*. So that has to be all right.'

'You didn't think I might be about to dump you?'

'No,' I say.

'Well, I was.'

I try to take this in. The point is, I don't get dumped. It's not something that happens. Then, suddenly, all sorts of premonitions of this moment start to come back to me. What had Daphne been trying to tell me that morning in Horsham, as I sat on the rose-embroidered bedspread? What did she say? 'Hugh liked you a lot. He'd always hoped that you and Virginia would get married, though I understand how things are now.' And what had cheered Virginia up so much outside the Internet cafe in Ambleside? What were these vague events at her work that had taken up so much of her time? As I may have said before, I just hate it when they do that thing where they take away your stomach and replace it (in this case) with a sack of cement.

'And are you still going to dump me?' I ask.

'Yes.'

'But . . .'

'I used to think you existed in your own little world, possibly believing that everything had been put there solely for your benefit. Now, of course, I know for certain that's what you believe. But even you must have seen this coming. There was a limit to how long I would be strung along, playing second fiddle to a clapped-out MG.'

'There's somebody else?'

'Sort of.'

'At work?'

'At work. It happens.'

I think of Lucy and the fact that nothing at all had happened there. On the other hand it is undeniable that elsewhere, unseen by me, such things do happen. Such things have always happened.

'And you were always planning to dump me as soon as we got back from Grasmere?' I say.

'Yes. Then, later, no. You were so *nice* to me. You didn't hesitate when I needed you to drive me to Horsham. You didn't hesitate when I needed you to drive me to Grasmere. You made my mother tea.'

'You changed your mind and decided you were going to spend the rest of your life with me because I made your mother tea?'

'That's how it works. It's all about small stuff. You're planning to dump your boyfriend but don't want to have to go to your best friend's wedding next week without a man and the right hat, so you go shopping for a hat and put off the dumping thing for a bit . . . a year later you're still together but can't remember why. Don't expect logic in any of it. And anyway, you said lovely things to me by Easedale Tarn. Harry wouldn't have done that. So I thought . . .'

Harry?

'Harry?' I say. 'Precisely who or what is this Harry?'

'Just a friend,' she lies.

'Just a friend?'

She shrugs. I'm going to find out about Harry soon enough. 'Anyway, I suppose I started to come round to the idea that – like my mother and Hugh – we'd just sort of end up together. Even that I'd rather like that. It wasn't as if Harry . . . well, it wasn't as if we were any more than friends, really. There would be some awkwardness at work, of course, when I told him . . .'

'Of course,' I say. 'I wouldn't want you to have awkwardness at work.' I don't like the note of bitterness in my voice, but I can see that it's there.

'So, I guess you and I would have stayed together,' she continues. 'We'd have got married. Converted my mother into a grandmother. Yes, it would have been a bit like Mum and Hugh, really. I can't tell you exactly what they felt for each other, but it worked well enough for them.'

'So, why not?' I demand. 'As you say, it worked for them.'

'Because *you* dumped *me*,' she says. 'By *email*. Up to that point I'd assumed that you, at least, had never wavered. You were loyal. I had a sort of duty to you. After all, I wasn't going to do to you what Jimmy did to me. But once I realized that you had doubts . . .'

'What if I'd proposed to you in Grasmere?'

'I'd have probably said OK.'

'So, I blew it?'

'Even as your fiancée, I might still have found your email a little odd.'

I suppose that's true. However I had phrased it, however bright the moon on the waters of Grasmere, it would all eventually have come back to that email.

'Chris,' she says, 'how old are you?'

(Silence.)

'How old are you?'

'Forty-two,' I say, not for the first time this week. What's this thing with my age all of a sudden?

'Forty-two,' she repeats. 'And how old do you act?'

(Silence)

'I'm thirty-two,' she says, 'but I feel like your older sister a lot of the time. Sometimes I feel like I'm your mother.'

'I've bought some socks,' I say.

'See – even now, you just want to turn everything into a one-liner. God, you're hopeless.'

I resist the temptation to turn everything into a one-liner.

'How old is Harry?' I ask. 'If he wants to settle down, he must be fifty at least.'

Virginia laughs. 'Twenty-nine,' she says. 'He's a bit of a puppy too. I don't learn, do I?'

Virginia reaches her hand out across the table. But I pull mine away.

'Look,' says Virginia, 'one day you'll meet somebody else. Somebody who will be better for you than I am. But when you do, promise me this: just try to be yourself. Don't pretend to be this beer-swilling moron. The real you is lovely. The person you pretend to be . . .'

'Yes?'

'. . . isn't.'

I say nothing, and she stretches out her hand in my direction again. It comes to rest in the middle of the empty table. There's nowhere else for it to go.

'I don't want sympathy,' I say. 'If that's it, if it's over, just clear off.'

'Can we be friends?'

'No.'

'I suppose there isn't any point in asking if you will be at the funeral?'

'You've got it in one,' I say.

'You wouldn't just be doing it for me. Couldn't you do it for Mum and Hugh?'

'No.'

She considers this. She clearly still thinks I should be there. 'Hugh always had a soft spot for you, even if he did take the piss out of you behind your back,' she says.

'Did he? Behind my back?'

'And to your face, but you never seemed to notice.' She pauses and bites her lip. 'Sorry – you didn't deserve that. Forget I said anything.'

'When did he take the piss out of me to my face?'

'Drop it. I didn't mean it.'

'I need to know.'

'OK – if that's what you want – he did it all the time really.'

'For example?'

'For example, there was that lunch when you were talking about Napoleon and Wellington, and obviously didn't know anything about either of them. He just thought you were a bit of a bullshitter, I suppose.'

'Thanks. That gives me a lot of encouragement to be at the funeral,' I say.

'OK, sorry – I said I shouldn't have told you. But it was

always good-natured. A bit like you and Dave, I would imagine. Hugh really liked you a lot. And in any case, my mother would want you to be there.'

'She'd probably settle for Harry in my place.'

'Yes, she's quite fond of him too,' says Virginia.

'She's met him?'

'She's met him.'

'So, she knows . . .'

'Yes,' she says.

'Brilliant. Bloody brilliant. Everyone knew except me.'

'Sorry.'

'Just go,' I say.

I am staring at the tabletop, so I don't actually see Virginia stand up, collect her small, neat handbag from the seat beside her and turn to go. I hear the familiar swish of her skirt and the click of her heels on the hard, cold floor. None of it has anything to do with me any more. The footsteps pause in their outward trajectory. She has turned to look at me, but I'll never be certain whether it is with annoyance or indifference or compassion or curiosity. It's not something I need to know. Then I hear the door thud and feel a rush of cool air against my skin.

It's over.

* * *

The walk back to the office seems to take for ever but that is still not long enough. I climb the stairs up to the highly prestigious first floor.

'Somebody phoned while you were out,' says Fatima, as

I try to avoid her gaze on my way in. 'Dave Birtwistle. He said you'd have his number. He said he was a friend of yours.'

'No friend of mine,' I say.

She gives a nervous giggle. She knows that half of what I say is intended as a joke, but is unsure which half.

'Fatima,' I say, 'am I just a lecherous, balding, middle-aged bastard?'

For a second she is too shocked to reply. 'Sorry?' she says. 'I don't understand.'

'I mean, is that the sort of thing that Lucy said about me?'

'Her skirts were far too short,' says Fatima with some feeling. 'She should not have worn things like that at work. Sometimes she did not wear . . . all of her underclothing. That is not good.'

It occurs to me that if she had not worn skirts like that, or had worn a bra, life might have been a bit easier. Or then again, maybe not. I'm learning about myself all the time.

'Ethics and Rights Committee?' says Fatima.

'What about them?'

'You're supposed to be there now.'

'Excellent. An opiate to numb the pain,' I say.

Fatima looks blank.

'I'm on my way,' I say.

* * *

The committee room looks out over the park. The sun is shining. Somewhere outside children are yelling at each other, kicking each other, having fun.

'. . . Chris?' the Chairman has just said to me.

I look up. 'Yes, of course,' I say.

This seems to be the right answer because he nods and continues: 'Since that is also Chris's view, we have no choice but to re-submit the terms of reference for the working party to Council, which will not be for two months . . .' He looks at me again and I nod. I have no idea when Council will be, nor do I care, but nodding is the line of least resistance.

'Mr Chairman, I really must protest,' a (bearded) committee member responds from the far end of the table. 'This is an important working party. A delay of two months is unacceptable.'

'I deplore Society bureaucracy as much as you do, but these things have to be properly approved if we want funding. I shall, however, talk to the President,' says the Chairman, 'and see if we can somehow short-circuit this. In the meantime, Chris, did you get a note of that action point?'

I look at the sheet of paper in front of me and see that I have written:

d

e

s

the mind slides

into emptiness

p

a

i

r

'Absolutely,' I say.

'Moving on,' says the Chairman, with a strange sideways glance at me. 'Item three. Now, I'd like to give a bit of time to this one.'

I look round the table and think: None of you exists. Not one. All I have to do is to call your bluff and you'll all vanish in a puff of smoke.

'. . . Chris?' says the Chairman. My attention has clearly wandered again.

'Yes,' I say.

This time, I have not got the right answer. There is a pause, then a sort of collective nervous laugh.

'It can't be both,' smiles the Chairman, 'however much the President would like to sit on the fence.' He seems to like me and is trying to pretend that I have been intentionally funny. 'So, Chris, do we go with the proposed government standard or stick with the UN Convention?'

I look at my agenda to see what on earth this can be about, but fortunately a number of committee members have strong views and take advantage of my silence to make them known. So I put my head in my hands and I think about Hugh and Virginia and Niels and Dave and how old I am, and I groan. Then I notice that the room has gone silent again.

'Chris clearly does not agree with that,' says the Chairman. He implies, however, that if I did not agree then I should have said it when invited to speak rather than moaned it later. He turns back to the previous speaker, but then somebody else says: 'No, Chris is right. We're making a meal of something that is actually very simple.'

The Chairman frowns. 'Is that what you think, Chris?'

I look from one to the other, and realize that I could very easily still get out of this with most of the committee still believing that I am sane and reasonably normal, but I also realize that I am in fact about to go for broke.

'This is,' I say, 'utterly pointless.'

They are all listening. The Chairman is looking at me very oddly, but several committee members nod in apparent agreement.

'What,' I ask them, 'is the point of it all? What are we all doing here?'

'As a committee, you mean?' interrupts somebody.

'He's right,' says somebody else. 'I've said over and over: all committees need proper work plans or they just drift. And that's just what this committee is doing.'

'*Is* that what you mean, Chris?' asks the Chairman. He's worried, though not as worried as he should be.

'What I mean,' I say, 'what I mean . . .'

At some point I have stood up – possibly with an idea of making a break for it, maybe just to get a better view of the proceedings. I am not too sure. There is a low rumble, which may be the noise of traffic outside in the street or may just be coming from inside my head. Possibly they are both the same place.

'What I mean,' I say for a third time, 'is that *none of you exists.*'

There, I've said it. I look round the room again, but strangely everyone is still there. I snap my fingers at them to see if that will do the trick, but it doesn't. Everyone is look-ing at me, some seem quite anxious, others merely curious to see what I will say next. I feel a bit like a car crash, with everyone standing around watching me, helpless. I think that my legs may be about to give way, but if that's what they want to do, then that's fine by me. I won't be needing them for a while.

There is the longest silence that I can ever recall, then I feel a hand on my shoulder, and I am being led from the room. As I am being gently pushed and guided through the doorway I glance back at the view of the park and think what a beautiful day it is. The intense blue of the sky, the intense green of the grass, the gentle motion of the tree branches. I don't think I've ever looked properly at any of this stuff before and it's all really, really beautiful.

28

A Nice Place, June Or Possibly July this Year

Everyone has been very kind to me.

The place that they sent me to is more like a hotel than a hospital. It is a large old house with simply acres of trees and lawns and flowers. I have a nice room with a comfortable bed, in which I get Plenty of Rest. They have told me: I can leave any time I wish. They have told me: if I want to, I could walk straight out between the big wrought-iron gates and down the dusty road to the nearest town – whatever it is. I am a voluntary patient. I don't have to stay here any more than you do. I really don't.

The doctors agree now that it is overwork. At first we talked a lot about the death of my parents and Niels, and how everything since then was my attempt to regain, not my childhood exactly, but that strange day when everything suddenly fell apart. But that didn't seem to lead anywhere much (as far as I was concerned anyway) so eventually we settled on overwork as the cause of my problems, which is obviously more straightforward to deal with. It's affecting lots of people, these days – loads – so it's an easy way to go. All I really need is Rest and a Chance to Sort Myself Out. And, as they point out to me, not everyone gets to come to somewhere like this.

Ironically, I am the first to benefit from the Society's new private healthcare insurance (rather than the gym membership I voted for). That's why I am in such a nice place. There are all sorts of famous people around – you'd have heard of them. Some like me are suffering from overwork and stress, others from drugs or alcohol in addition to (or more often in place of) work. There's an actor who was in one of the soaps until they killed him off, which is sort of why he is here now, trying to get over the death of his other self. There's somebody who was in a rock band back in the eighties (but not any more) and somebody who came fourth or fifth in *Big Brother* a while back and couldn't handle the success. Sometimes I sit with them in the garden and we talk about why we are here and what we are going to do when we leave here – which, as I say, we could all do at any time, though it might frighten the people in the next town (whatever it is) if we all did it at once.

Sometimes people come to see me. Narinder comes quite often and tells me what is happening at the Society. He's getting married soon to a girl from Amritsar. He's very happy about it. They've given Jon my old job but they haven't bothered to fill Lucy's post because nobody can work out what it was that she did, except wear short skirts and tight sweaters. They've appointed an external candidate to replace Roger when he leaves. Brindley Passmore threatened to resign when he didn't become Secretary, but he's still there. Brindley has never been in to see me, but he did write, HR being one of his responsibilities. He says they'll try to find me another job when I leave here – not my old one, obviously, but something less stressful, and possibly part-time to begin with. It's called a Phased Return to Work. The Society have even sent somebody in to check my flat from time to time and make sure that the bills are picked up and paid. They tell me everything is OK, but they were worried that somebody had tried to vandalize one of the wing mirrors of my car.

Virginia hasn't been to see me either. She's probably busy. Of course, I never did get to Hugh's funeral, any more than Malcolm did.

I don't think I'll go to David and Megan's wedding either, though they have kindly sent me a beautifully printed invitation with gold edging and said that they very much hope I will be well enough to come. David had slipped in a note saying, *'Hope you're feeling better, mate. See you soon. My round!'* That was nice of him.

I think that the doctors stopped talking to me about my childhood, and started talking about stress management, mainly because they saw that I had come to terms with the way Niels had died and no longer needed to question reality. All of which shows you can fool anyone if you try hard enough and, deep down, they want to be fooled. If they think I am happy, then from their perspective I am happy. And if I am happy then they've done their job. *Esse est percipi,* as somebody once said. Within their own reality, I am well on my way to recovery.

And – do you know? – I really *am* happy. I know now

that I should be pleased to be alive rather than guilty not to have been in a car smash twenty years ago. I am looking forward to accepting responsibility and acting my age. I shall most certainly buy socks.

So, thank you for your concern, and don't think I'm ungrateful, but actually I'm fine. I hope you never have to go through the sort of stuff I've been through, but if you do, then I hope you come out the other side, just as I have.

If you exist, of course. If you exist.

Acknowledgments

My thanks to everyone at Macmillan, but especially Will, Sophie, Maria, Caitriona, Ellen and Mary (not to mention O'Hara) for their help, for their collective faith in me and for making this a much better book.

My thanks for support and encouragement on the way to (amongst others) Helen, Krish, Susan-the-Archivist, Rhian, Dave and Daniel at Goldsboro Books, Martin and Angela (who own a real and highly recommended guest house on the site of my fictitious one) and all of my fellow writers at MNW.

Above all I am grateful to Ann, Tom and Catrin for their patience while I was working on this (and other books). And finally my thanks to Thistle for total devotion and the occasional dead rabbit.

The quotation from *Think* by Simon Blackburn (OUP 1999) appears by permission of the Oxford University Press.